Anonymous

A Collection of Original Poems

By the Rev. Mr Blacklock, and other Scotch gentlemen

Anonymous

A Collection of Original Poems
By the Rev. Mr Blacklock, and other Scotch gentlemen

ISBN/EAN: 9783337409630

Printed in Europe, USA, Canada, Australia, Japan

Cover: Foto ©Andreas Hilbeck / pixelio.de

More available books at **www.hansebooks.com**

A

COLLECTION

OF

ORIGINAL POEMS.

BY

The Rev. Mr BLACKLOCK, and other
SCOTCH GENTLEMEN.

EDINBURGH:

Printed for A. DONALDSON, at Pope's Head;
and fold by R. and J. DODSLEY in Pall-Mall, and
J. RICHARDSON in Pater-noster-row, *London*.

MDCCLX.

ADVERTISEMENT.

IT was the editor's intention to have given three volumes of original poems at once; but, at the defire of thofe gentlemen to whom the public are indebted for the following collection, this firft volume is offered as a fpecimen of the whole.

It is not to be expected, that, in a mifcellaneous collection, every poem will be found of equal merit, and to pleafe every reader, mens taftes differing as much as their faces. Mean time no piece has been inferted in this volume without a critical examination by gentlemen of tafte and character.

The editor takes this opportunity of making his acknowledgments to feveral gentlemen for their friendly contributions for this volume, in particular to the Rev. Mr BLACK-LOCK, and Mr GORDON; and begs that other gentlemen, friends to the Mufes, will give their affiftance for the volumes intended to follow.

Perfors poffeffed of original pieces, are defired to communicate them to the editor; which, if approved, fhall be inferted in the fecond and third volumes.

CONTENTS.

The

  Cupid

A

COLLECTION

OF

ORIGINAL POEMS.

✥✥✥✥✥✥✥✥✥✥✥✥✥✥✥✥✥✥✥✥✥✥✥✥✥✥✥✥✥✥✥✥

To TWO SISTERS on their
WEDDING-DAY.

An EPISTLE.

By Mr BLACKLOCK.

DEAR Ladies, whilſt the nuptial hour at hand
Muſt all your time, and all your thoughts de-
mand,
Though all the Nine my tuneful ſtrain inſpir'd,
My heart though all the force of friendſhip fir'd,
Though warm'd with tranſport for my lovely theme,
I wou'd not long your kind attention claim ;
Yet let me join the gratulating throng,
And breathe to Heav'n one ardent wiſh in ſong :
That all your future days, ſerene and bright,
May flow diſtinguiſh'd by ſincere delight ;

A   That

That full fuccefs your wifhes may attend,
And Heav'n's beft bleffings on your heads defcend;
That love and joy may on each period wait,
While hoary Time unrolls the page of fate;
Till all who hear your deftiny admire,
Nore more from Heav'n to make them blefs'd require;
Till tender mothers, who your lot furvey,
Thus in the fondnefs of their fouls fhall pray :
" May my fair daughter, or my fav'rite fon,
" Be blefs'd, and live and love as thefe have done."

+-+

Eftimate of H U M A N G R E A T N E S S.

In imitation of a French epigram.

By the fame.

ONE night I dream'd, and dreams may oft prove true,
That to this foolifh world I bade adieu.
With folemn rites, and decent grief deplor'd,
My friends to mother-earth her gift reftor'd.
But O ! eternal infult to my fhade,
Clofe by a vile plebeian corfe was laid !
Enrag'd, confin'd, I try'd to fhift my ground ;
But all attempts were unfuccefsful found.
Be gone, grofs lump, I cry'd, in high difdain,
No flave of abject birth fhall here remain.
Be diftant far — to nobler names gives way,
And mix with vulgar duft thy fordid clay.

Thou

Thou fool! thou wretch! a hollow voice reply'd,
Now learn the impotence of wealth and pride;
Hereditary names and honours, here,
With all their farce and tinfel difappear.
In thefe dark realms, Death's reptile heralds trace
From one fole origin all human race:
On all the line one equal lot attends;
From duft it rifes, and to duft defcends.
Here pale Ambition, quitting pomp and form,
Admits her laft — beft counfellor, a worm.
Here Nature's charter ftands confirm'd alone;
The grave is lefs precarious than the throne.
Then feek not here pre-eminence and ftate,
But own and blefs th' impartial will of Fate;
With life, its errors, and its whims refign,
Nor think a beggar's title worfe than thine.

To her Grace the DUCHESS of HAMIL-TON, on her recovery from child-bed, after the birth of the MAR-QUIS of CLYDESDALE.

By the fame.

HAil! Nature's lovelieft work and darling care,
Whofe worth and beauty equal praifes claim,
Form'd Heav'n's fupreme beneficence to fhare,
A nation's wonder, and a mother's name.

No

No venal mufe with mercenary praife,
  Infults thy tafte, or wounds thy modeft ear ;
When Heav'n, or heav'nly beauty prompts her lays,
  As high the theme, the tribute flows fincere.

Blefs'd be the hours, which, with aufpicious flight,
  Reftore thy former health and native bloom ;
To bid the wifhing world its eyes delight,
  And Fame, with all her mouths, thy praife refume.

O may the infant product of thy pain,
  Beyond a mother's wifh to greatnefs rife ;
The cloudlefs glories of his race fuftain,
  On earth belov'd, and honour'd in the fkies.

Fraught with the richeft, nobleft gifts of fate,
  Serenely gay may all thy moments roll ;
To crown thy days let ev'ry pleafure wait,
  Bright as thy charms, and fpotlefs as thy foul.

✤✤✤✤✤✤✤✤ ✤✤✤✤✤✤✤✤✤✤✤✤✤✤✤✤✤✤✤✤✤✤ ✤✤✤✤✤✤

ODE on a favourite LAP-DOG.

To Mifs G—— J——.

By the fame.

PRetty, fportive, happy creature,
  Full of life, and full of play,
Taught to live by faithful Nature,
  Never canft thou mifs thy way.

By

By her dictates kind inftructed,
  Thou avoid'ft each real fmart;
We, by other rules conducted,
  Lofe our joy to fhow our art.

Undifguis'd, each reigning paffion
  When thou mov'ft or look'ft we fee;
Were the fame with us the fafhion,
  Happy mortals would we be!

May her favour ftill purfue thee,
  Who propos'd thee for my theme;
Till fuperior charms fubdue thee,
  And infpire a nobler flame.

In each other blefs'd and bleffing,
  Years of pleafure let them live;
Each all active worth poffeffing,
  Earth admires, or Heav'n can give.

✢✤✢✤✢✤✢✤ ✤✢✤✢✤✢✤✢✤✢✤✢✤✢✤✢✤✢✤✢✤✢ ✤✢✤✢

To a fuccefsful rival, who faid ironically, he pitied the author.

An ODE.

By the fame.

THou pity! fond unthinking boy,
  Falfely elate with diftant joy,

Did

Did e'er thy heart the kind emotion know,
Th' endearing pangs of fympathetic wo!

Yes; as on Nile's prolific fhore,
The monfters, cloy'd with recent gore,
Sad o'er the reeking carnage howling lie,
Such tears, fincere as thine, o'erflow the murd'rer's eye.

O loft to virtue! loft to fhame!
Beneath fair Friendfhip's holy name,
Impious to tempt, and fubtle to betray,
While heav'n and earth the daring crime furvey.

What devil arm'd thy front with fteel,
To feign a grief thou ne'er couldft feel;
Without a blufh, the faithlefs figh to heave,
And mourn the mortal ftab thy own curs'd dagger gave?

But if to Heav'n's impartial throne,
The piercing figh and bitter groan,
For juft redrefs, on angel-wings arife, .
Then dread the blafting vengeance of the fkies.

Ah, where will rage my foul impell?
How high the tide of fury fwell?
Fool! thus to curfe the man whofe ev'ry fmart
Muft pierce thy inmoft foul, muft wound Clarinda's
heart.

CATO

Cato Uticensis to his wife at Rome.

By the same.

IN diftant regions, Freedom's laft retreat,
Where Rome and fhe their final crifis wait,
Cato reflects how much he once was bleft,
And greets with health the fav'rite of his breaft.

Oh! when my foul with retrofpective eyes
Beholds each fcene of paft enjoyment rife,
Ere vice and Heav'n's irrevocable doom
Shook the firm bafis of imperial Rome,
What horrors muft this patriot heart congeal!
What muft a father and an hufband feel!
Ye moments, deftin'd to eternal flight,
Who fhone on each domeftic bleffing bright,
Who faw me with eaith's legiflators join'd,
Balance the facred rights of human kind,
No more my foul your blefs'd return muft know,
Confign'd to fetters, infamy and wo;
Expell'd from Rome, and all that's dear, we fly
Through fruitlefs deferts, and a flaming fky,
Where thunders roar inceffant, lightnings glare,
And plagues unnumber'd taint the boundlefs air;
Where ferpents, children of eternal night,
Enfure perdition with their mortal bite;
Where burning fands to heav'n in furges roll,
And fcorching heats evaporate the foul.

Yet

Yet pleas'd thefe harfh extremes of fate we bear;
For Liberty, Heav'n's nobleft gift, is here.
Unaw'd by pow'r, from venal fhackles free,
Our hands accomplifh what our hearts decree.
Yet here, where anguifh, want, and horror reign,
The heav'nly power explores a feat in vain.
Ambitious blood-hounds hold her clofe in view,
Faithful to fcent, and active to purfue.
See o'er the fpacious globe their courfe they bend;
See conqueft and fuccefs their fteps attend.
Oceans in vain to ftop their paffage flow,
And mountains rife in everlafting fnow.
Obfequious billows own tyrannic fway,
And ftorms have learn'd to flatter and obey.
Eternal Pow'rs! whofe will is Nature's guide,
Who o'er high heav'n and earth and hell prefide,
Muft then that plan of liberty expire,
Which patriot bofoms more than life defire?
Is public happinefs for ever fled,
For which the fage explor'd and hero bled?
Shall Pompey's blood the coaft of Egypt ftain?
Shall civil flaughter load Pharfalia's plain?
With reeking gore fhall plunder'd temples flow?
Is Jove or Cæfar god of all below?
Be curs'd the time when Pleafure and her train,
O'er Rome extended firft their fatal reign;
For O! 'twas then, in that detefted hour,
That firft the luft of treafure and of power
From public welfare could our views divert,
And quench each virtue in the human heart.

The genealogy of NONSENSE.

An EPISTLE.

By the same.

DEAR MADAM,

With long and careful fcrutiny, in vain
    I fearch'd th' obfcure receffes of my brain;
The mufes oft with mournful plaints I woo'd,
To find excufe for filence, if they cou'd.
But through my fearch not one excufe appear'd,
And not a mufe would anfwer, if fhe heard.

Thus I remain'd in anxious fad fufpenfe,
Defpairing aid from reafon or from fenfe;
Till from a pow'r, of late well known to fame,
Though not invok'd, the wifh'd folution came.

Now Night incumbent hung o'er half the ball,
And Silence fpread her empire over all;
When o'er my eyes imperfect flumbers fpread
Their downy wings, and hover'd round my head:
But ftill internal fenfe awake remain'd,
And ftill its firft folicitude retain'd;
When lo! with flow defcent, obfcurely bright,
And cloth'd in darknefs vifible, not light,
A form, high tow'ring to the azure fkies,
In ftupid grandeur rofe before my eyes.

A 3

As after ſtorms waves faintly laſh the ſhore,
As hollow winds in rocky caverns roar;
Such was the voice which pierc'd my trembling ear,
And chill'd my ſoul with more than common fear.

Thus ſpoke the power: " From you extended void,
" Where Jove's creating hand was ne'er employ'd;
" Where ſoft with hard, and heavy mix'd with light,
" And hot with cold, maintain eternal fight;
" Where end the realms of order, form, and day,
" Where Night and Chaos hold primeval ſway;
" Their firſt, their darling offspring now explore,
" Who comes thy wonted calmneſs to reſtore.
" Ere yet the mountains rear'd their heads on high,
" Ere yet the radiant ſun illum'd the ſky;
" Ere riſing hills or humble vales were ſeen,
" Or woods the proſpect chear'd with waving green;
" Ere Nature was, my wondrous birth I date,
" More old than Chance, Neceſſity, or Fate;
" Ere yet the muſes touch'd the vocal lyre,
" My rev'rend mother, and tumultuous ſire,
" Beheld my wondrous birth, with vaſt amaze,
" And Diſcord's boundleſs empire roar'd my praiſe.

" In me whate'er by nature is disjoin'd,
" All oppoſite extremes involv'd you find.
" Born to retain by Fate's eternal doom,
" My ſire's confuſion, and my mother's gloom;
" O'er all the vaſt extent of letter'd pride,
" With uncontroll'd dominion I preſide;
" Through its deep gloom I dart the doubtful ray,
" And teach the learned idiots where to ſtray:
" The

" The labouring chymiſt, and profound divine,
" Err, not ſeduc'd by Reaſon's light, but mine :
" From me alone *theſe* boaſt the wondrous ſkill,
" To make a myſtery more myſterious ſtill ;
" While *thoſe* purſue, by ſcience not their own,
" The univerſal cure, and philoſophic ſtone.
" Thus when the leaden pedant courts my aid,
" To cover ignorance with learning's ſhade,
" To ſwell the folio to a proper ſize,
" And throw the clouds of art o'er nature's eyes ;
" My ſoporific pow'r the ſages own ;
" Hence by the ſacred name of *Dulneſs* known.
" But if mercurial ſcribblers pant for fame,
" Thoſe I inſpire, and NONSENSE is my name.
" Suſtain'd by me, thy muſe firſt took her flight,
" I circumſcribe its limits and its height ;
" By me ſhe ſinks, by me ſhe ſoars along ;
" I rule her ſilence, and I prompt her ſong."

My doubts reſolv'd, the goddeſs wing'd her flight,
Diſſolv'd in air, and mix'd with formleſs Night.
Much more the muſe reluctant muſt ſupprefs,
For all the pow'r of Time and Fate confeſs :
Too ſoft her accents, and too weak her pray'r,
For Time, or Fate, or cruel poſts to hear.

T. B.

February 22. 1758.

    Thurſday.

The poſt was juſt at that inſtant going to ſet off.

Aɲ

An ELEGY.

Infcribed to C—— S——, Efq;

By the fame.

O Friend, by ev'ry fympathy endear'd,
  Which foul with foul in facred ties unite,
The hour arrives, fo long, fo juftly fear'd,
  Brings all its woes, and finks me with their weight,

For now from heav'n my unavailing pray'r
  Tofs'd devious mingles with the fportive gale ;
No tender arts can move my cruel fair,
  Nor all Love's filent eloquence prevail.

Though from my lips no found unmeaning flows,
  Though in each action fondnefs is expreft,
No kind returns e'er terminate my woes,
  Nor heave th' eternal preffure from my breaft.

Too well the weaknefs of my heart I knew,
  Too well Love's pow'r my foul had felt before;
Why did I then the pleafing ill purfue,
  And tempt the malice of my fate once more?

Confcious how few amongft the fair fucceed,
  Who boaft no merit but a tender heart,
Why was my foul again to chains decreed,
  To unrewarded tears, and endlefs fmart?

The

The firen Hope, my tardy pace to chear,
  In gay prefage the fhort'ning profpect dreft,
With art fallacious brought the object near,
  And lull'd each rifing doubt in fatal reft.

I faw Succefs, or thought at leaft I faw,
  Beck'ning with fmiles to animate my fpeed:
Reafon was mute, imprefs'd with trembling awe;
  Nor Memory one precedent cou'd plead.

How curs'd is he who never learn'd to fear
  The keeneft plagues his cruel ftars portend!
Till o'er his head the black'ning clouds appear,
  And heav'n's collected ftorms at once defcend.

What further change of fortune can I wait?
  What confummation to the laft defpair?
She flies, yet fhows no pity for my fate;
  She fees, yet deigns not in my griefs to fhare.

Yet the kind heart where tender paffions reign,
  Will catch the foftnefs when it firft appears,
Explore each fymptom of the fuff'rer's pain,
  Sigh all his fighs, and number all his tears.

This tribute from humanity is due,
  What then, juft Heav'ns! what fhould not love be-
    ftow?
Yet though the fair infenfible I view,
  For others blifs I wou'd not change my woe.

O blind to wifdom! to reflection blind,
   At length to reafon and thyfelf return;
See Science wait thee with reception kind,
   Whofe frown or abfence no fond lovers mourn.

Bounteous and free to all who afk her aid,
   Her facred light anticipates their call,
Points out the precipice to which they ftray'd,
   And with maternal care prevents their fall.

Daughter of God! whofe features all exprefs
   Th' eternal beauty whence thy being fprung,
I to thy facred fhrine my fteps addrefs,
   And catch each found from thy heav'n-prompted tongue.

O take me wholly to thy fond embrace,
   Through all my foul thy heav'nly beams effufe!
Thence ev'ry cloud of pleafing error chafe,
   Adjuft her organs, and enlarge her views.

Hence ever fix'd on virtue and on thee,
   No lower wifh fhall her attention claim,
Till, like her facred parent, pure and free,
   She rife to native heaven from whence fhe came.

The

The chronicle of a HEART.

In imitation of COWLEY.

By the fame.

I.

HOW often my heart has by love been o'erthrown,
   What grand revolutions its empire has known,
You aſk me, dear friend; then attend the ſad ſtrain,
Since you bid me renew ſuch ineffable pain.
   Derry down, down, hey derry down.

II.

For who that has got e'er an eye in his pate,
So diſmal a tale without tears can relate;
Or who ſuch dire annals recall to his mind,
Without burſting in ſighs, both before and behind?

III.

This kingdom, as authors impartial have told,
At firſt was elective, but afterwards ſold;
For experience will ſhow whoe'er pleaſes to try,
That kingdoms are venal when ſubjects can buy.

IV.

Lovely Peggy, the firſt in ſucceſſion and name,
Was early inveſted with honour ſupreme;
But a bold ſon of Mars, who grew fond of her form,
Swore himſelf into grace, and ſurpris'd her by ſtorm.

B 2   V.

V.

Maria fucceeded in honour and place,
By laughing and fqueezing, and fong and grimace;
But her favours, alas, like her carriage, were free,
Beftow'd on the whole male creation but me.

VI.

Next Marg'ret the fecond attempted the chace;
Though the fmall pox and age had enamell'd her face,
She fuftain'd her pretence *fans merite et fans teix*,
And carried her point by a *Je ne fçais quoi.*

VII.

The heart which fo tamely acknowledg'd her fway,
Still fuffer'd in filence, and kept her at bay,
Till old Time had at laft fo much mellow'd her charms,
That fhe dropt with a breeze in a liv'ryman's arms.

VIII.

The next eafy conqueft, Belinda, was thine,
Obtain'd by the mufical tinkle of coin:
But fhe, more enamour'd of fport than of prey,
Had a fifh in her hook which fhe wanted to play.

IX.

High hopes were her baits; but if truth were confefs'd,
A good ftill in profpect is not good poffefs'd;
For the fool found too late he had taken a tartar,
Retreated with wounds, and begg'd ftoutly for quarter.

X.

X.

Urania came next, and with fubtle addrefs,
Difcover'd no open attempts to poffefs :
But when fairly admitted, of conqueft fecure,
She acknowledg'd no law but her will and her pow'r.

XI.

For feven tedious years, to get rid of her chain,
All force prov'd abortive, all ftratagem vain,
Till a youth with much fatnefs and gravity bleft,
Her perfon detain'd by a lawful arreft.

XII.

To a reign fo defpotic, though guiltlefs of blood,
No wonder a long interregnum enfu'd ;
For an afs, though the patienteft brute of the plain,
Once jaded and gall'd, will beware of the rein.

XIII.

Now the kingdom ftands doubtful itfelf to furrender,
To Cloe the fprightly, or Celia the flender :
But if once it were out of this pitiful cafe,
No law but the Salic henceforth fhall take place.

*Moft of the characters here defcribed are real, but
the paffions fictitious.*

An

An E L E G Y on the anniverſary of the DEATH of a FRIEND.

By ————

Inſcribed to Mr BLACKLOCK.

I.

TO pious ſorrow ſacred be this day,
    By grief diſtinguiſh'd each revolving year;
Still let me form the melancholy lay,
    And pay the tribute of a gentle tear.

II.

Let happier poets, prodigal of wo,
    With fancy'd ſorrows ſwell the pompous ſtrain,
Mourn like ſome heart-exulting heir, for ſhow ;
    I wiſh but to deſcribe my real pain.

III.

Why was he form'd (ah, why) ſo ſweet of ſoul,
    Serene and gentle as a ſummer's ſky ?
Why did he reach ſo ſoon the deſtin'd goal,
    Born juſt to make his value known, and die ?

IV.

Thus in the morn the lily rears its head,
    Unfolds its fragrant beauties to the ſkies ;
Fairer than ſnow its virgin leaves are ſpread ;
    But ere 'tis noon it hangs its head and dies.

V.

V.

In vain fair Science op'd her richeſt ſtore,
    And Learning grac'd, and Genius bloom'd in vain;
Learning, alas! nor Genius have the pow'r
    To ſhield one hour the human clay from pain.

VI.

Whene'er with him my happier days I paſt,
    Heedleſs I mark'd not how the ſeaſons grew;
Swift fled the jocund hours with blithſome haſte,
    And ſcatter'd ſweets ambroſial as they flew.

VII.

Then the young Spring in verdant mantle dreſt,
    Summer's unclouded ſkies and ſpreading trees,
Autumn's brown fields with ripen'd harveſts bleſt,
    And Winter's rattling tempeſts then could pleaſe.

VIII.

But now, to Sorrow's edge a moping prey,
    Dull as hoar Age, e'en in my growing prime,
I chide each hour protracted to a day;
    Grief, ſurely Grief arreſts the wings of Time.

IX.

Spring's op'ning charms, and Summer's ripen'd bloom,
    Autumn's brown fields, and Winter's low'ring brow,
Alike unheeded now, unwiſh'd for come;
    Alike untaſted, unregretted go.

X.

X.

'Twas he, 'twas he, made ev'ry feafon gay,
  Tinged each flower with beauties not its own ;
'Twas his to drefs in fmiles the blackeft day ;
  But fmiles are now no more —— for he is gone.

XI.

Shed, virgins, fhed the fympathifing tear,
  You who deferve a tender virgin's name ;
A youth untimely. prefs'd the fatal bier,
  Soft as your foul, and fpotlefs as your fame.

XII.

And wilt thou, BLACKLOCK, grant the boon I crave ?
  (As I each year his mournful tale relate),
Wilt thou ftrow annual flow'rs upon his grave,
  Sweet as his temper, early as his fate ?

✤✤✤✤✤✤✤✤✤✤✤✤✤✤✤✤✤✤✤✤✤✤✤✤✤✤✤✤✤✤✤✤✤✤✤✤✤

TO A LADY.

With HAMMOND'S ELEGIES.

By ——

O Form'd at once to feel, and to infpire
  The nobleft paffions of the human breaft,
Attend the accents of Love's fav'rite lyre,
  And let thy foul its moving force atteft.

The foul of paffion in each found convey'd,
　Shall all its joy difclofe, and all its fmart,
Reafon to decent tendernefs perfuade,
　Smooth ev'ry thought, and humanize the heart.

Falfe is that wifdom, impotent and vain,
　Which fcorns the fphere by Heav'n to men affign'd;
Which treats Love's pureft fires with mock difdain,
　And, human, foars above the human kind.

Long mute the mufe of Elegy remain'd,
　Her plaints untaught by nature to renew,
Whilft fportive Wit delufive forrows feign'd,
　With how much eafe diftinguifh'd from the true!

Ev'n witty Waller mourns the conftant fcorn
　Of Sachariffa, and his fate, in vain:
With love his fancy, not his heart feems torn;
　We praife his wit, but cannot fhare his pain.

Such force has Nature, fo fupremely fair,
　With charms maternal, her productions fhine;
The eafy grace and animated air,
　Proclaim them all her own, and all divine.

O! fhould fuch merit in fuch ftrains implore,
　Let Beauty ftill vouchfafe a gentle ear;
What can the foul with paffion touch'd do more?
　The fong muft prove the fentiment fincere.

Cold Cunning ne'er, with animated ſtrain,
  To other breaſts can warmth unfelt impart;
We ſee her toil with induſtry and pain,
  And mock the painted impotence of Art.

✢✢✢✢✢✢✢✢✢✢✢✢✢✢✢✢✢✢✢✢✢✢✢✢✢✢✢✢✢✢✢✢✢✢✢✢✢✢

S O N G.

Inſcribed to a F R I E N D.

In imitation of S H E N S T O N E.

By Mr B L A C K L O C K.

I.

CEaſe, ceaſe, my dear friend, to explore
    From whence, and how piercing my ſmart;
Let the charms of the nymph I adore,
  Excuſe, and interpret my heart:
Then how much I admire, you ſhall prove,
  When like me you are taught to admire;
And imagine how boundleſs my love;
  When you number the charms that inſpire.

II.

Than ſunſhine more dear to my ſight,
  To my life more eſſential than air,
To my ſoul ſhe is perfect delight,
  To my ſenſe all that's pleaſing and fair.

The

The fwains who her beauty behold,
　With tranfport applaud ev'ry charm,
And fwear that the breaft muft be cold,
　Which a beam fo intenfe cannot warm.

III.

Ah! fay, will fhe flightly forego
　A conqueft, though humble, yet fure?
Will fhe leave a poor fhepherd to wo,
　Who for her ev'ry blifs would procure?
Alas! too prefaging my fears,
　Too jealous my foul of its blifs;
Methinks fhe already appears,
　To forefee, and elude my addrefs.

IV.

Does my boldnefs offend my dear maid?
　Is my fondnefs loquacious and free?
Are my vifits too frequently paid;
　Or my converfe unworthy of thee?
Yet when grief was too big for my breaft,
　And labour'd in fighs to complain,
Its ftruggles I oft have fuppreft,
　And filence impos'd on my pain.

V.

And oft, while, by tendernefs caught,
　To my charmer's retirement I flew,
I reproach'd the fond abfence of thought,
　And in blufhing confufion withdrew.

My

My fpeech, though too little refin'd,
Though fimple and aukward my mien;
Yet ftill, fhouldft thou deign to be kind,
What a wonderful change might be feen!

VI.

Ah, Strephon! how vain thy defire,
Thy numbers and mufic how vain,
While merit and fortune confpire
The fmiles of the nymph to obtain?
Yet ceafe to upbraid the foft choice,
Though it ne'er fhould determine for thee,
If thy heart in her joy may rejoice,
Unhappy thou never canft be.

✥✚✛✚✛✚✥✚✛✚✛✛✚✥✛✛✛✚✥ ✛✚✥✚✛✛✥ ✚✛✚✥✥✚ ✥✚✛✛✥✚✥

H O R. Ode 13. Book 1. imitated.

By the fame.

Cum tu, Lydia, Telephi, &c.

WHen Celia dwells on Damon's name,
Infatiate of the pleafing theme;
Or in detail admires his charms,
His rofy neck and waxen arms;
O! then with fury fcarce fuppreft,
My big heart labours in my breaft.

From

From thought to thought, my starting soul,
Inceffant tides of paffion roll;
My blood alternate chills and glows,
Uncertain colour comes and goes;
While down my cheek the filent tear,
Too plainly bids my grief appear;
Too plainly fhows the latent flame,
Whofe flow confumption melts my frame.
I burn when, confcious of his fway,
The youth elated I furvey;
Prefume with infolence of air,
To frown, or dictate to my fair;
Or in the madnefs of delight
When to thy arms he wings his flight,
And, with indelicate embrace,
Profanes the beauty of that face;
That face, where op'ning Heav'n beftows,
The brighteft charms with which it glows.
O! if my counfels touch thine ear,
Love's counfel ever is fincere,
From his indecent tranfports fly,
Howe'er his form may pleafe thine eye.
For conflagrations fierce and ftrong
Are fatal ftill, but never long:
And he who rudely treats the fhrine
Where modeft worth and beauty fhine,
Forgetful of his former fire,
Shall foon no more thefe charms admire.
How blefs'd! how more than blefs'd are they!
Whom Love retains with equal fway;

Whofe

Whofe flame inviolably bright,
Still burns in its meridian height:
Nor jealous fears, nor cold difdain,
Difturb their peace, nor break their chain;
But when the hours of life are paft,
For each in fighs they breathe their laft.

On the cultivation of TASTE,

An EPISTLE.

To a young Lady.

By Mr G.————

The CONTENTS.

His

His Pastorals 104. *His style and numbers in general*
111. *Addison's character as a poet and patriot* 124.
*Digression to the Spectator, which is described as
proper to improve the mind, entertain the fancy,
cultivate the taste, and form the style of a young per-
son* 136. *Thomson's character as a poet* 145.
Young's Universal Passion described 154. *Garth's
Dispensatory and Clariment* 158. *Swift's character
for wit, humour, ill-nature, and want of delicacy*
170. *Short characters of Gay, Prior, Parnell,
Hammond, Welsh, Shenstone, Gray, Lyttelton, Blacklock* 186. *Here the author leaves the lady to her own
choice in poetry* 192. *A caution not to confine her
reading to poetry alone* 195. *The advantages which
attend the study of history.——The histories of Greece
and Rome, and that of Britain, recommended* 204. *A
notion of moral and natural philosophy not improper.
——Shaftesbury's and Nettleton's short treatises point-
ed out for the first, and Nature displayed for the
last* 216. *A recommendation to employ her leisure
hours in reading, though some absurdly would confine
all knowledge to the other sex* 222. *A caution against
letting speculation ingross all her thoughts. Those active and social virtues recommended which are adapted
to her nature, sex, and station* 240. *The above duties consistent with taste and knowledge. This exem-
plified in the characters of Madam Dacier and Mrs
Rowe* 245. *Such examples likewise amongst ourselves
hinted at.—— Conclusion.*

MY

MY dear ZELINDA, since you would explore
What verses I at present have in store,
Receive inclos'd some unconnected rhymes,
The work of various hands, at various times.

Your dawning taste with pleasure I survey,   5
And to its search would nobler scenes display;
Nor still to manuscripts confine your views,
The careless sallies of the sporting muse :
But fix your eye where real beauty reigns,
And public sanction dignifies the strains..   10

From Nature's charms supreme delight to share,
To feel what's good — sublime — or new — or fair,
With higher prospects fires the human aim,
Refines our pleasures, and improves our frame :
This task the muses claim, by Heav'n design'd   15
The heart to soften, and enlarge the mind ;.

Verf. 5. *Your dawning taste,* &c.
    The lady's age fifteen.

Verf. 12 *To feel what's good,* &c.
    Novelty, goodness, beauty, and grandeur or sublimity, are
the sources from whence all the pleasures of the internal senses
are derived.

Verf. 15. *This task the muses,* &c.
    The muses preside alike over all the polite arts; but music,
painting, and sculpture, contribute in some degree to the same
end with poetry.—— It has been disputed, which of the imita-
tions are most productive of improvement; but, upon the whole,
the preference seems due to poetry.——See Harris on that subject..

At once to guide and animate our way,
Where Truth and Virtue hold eternal fway.
Thefe glorious ends effectually to gain,
They charm the ear, the fancy entertain ;   20
Paint all that's fair in Nature to the fight,
And mix fublime inftruction with delight.

Yet not alone this tafk the Mufe effays ;
Pretending firens oft ufurp her praife,
Deck with delufive charms the mimic lay,   25
And lead too foon th' unwary mind aftray.
Hence, though in Mufic all her numbers flow,
Through all her fong though endlefs raptures glow,
Let Tafte, let Virtue fly th' inchanting ftrain ;
Where falfe the fentiment, the joy is vain.   30

Not each affuming bard the Nine infpire,
Whofe facrilegious hand profanes the lyre.
Where-e'er the fong to faithlefs Pleafure leads,
Through fairy profpects or illufive meads,
Or flows in dull unanimated rhyme,   35
To meannefs finks, or fwells to mock fublime ;
The quaint conceit, the force of lab'ring art,
Can to the Mufe or Nature owe no part.

Let HOMER ftill your firft attention claim,
Whom all the Nine, with all their charms, inflame.   40

Verf. 37. *The quaint conceit,* &c.
    Almoft all the wits in Charles II.'s time may be ranged under
this clafs, when even grave divines vouchfafed to be jocular,
and threw their puns and quibbles from the pulpit.

                                                        He

He firſt eſſay'd their nobleſt wreaths to gain:
Ambitious taſk! yet not eſſay'd in vain.
Him future bards with veneration view,
And with unequal wing his flights purſue;
From him Invention's copious ſource explore,   45
And deck their labours with the borrow'd ſtore.

To find a hand that durſt attempt his ſtrain,
A thouſand toiling years revolv'd in vain;
Till Fate and Nature ſmiling on mankind,
Another brow for epic bays deſign'd,   50
Deſtin'd beneath Heſperian ſuns to bloom,
And ſhine the glory of the world and Rome.
Hail ſacred MARO! in whoſe deathleſs ſtrain,
Nature and Art united praiſe attain:
Correct and pure thy heav'nly numbers flow,   55
Yet with the keeneſt flame of Genius glow;
Through all the records of eternal Fate,
Fame ſaw but one of Nature's works ſo great.

Britannia's boaſt! whoſe lyre, by angels ſtrung,
Reſounded equal to the themes he ſung!   60
That man his nature might with pleaſure ſee,
In its full height, — God ſaid, Let MILTON be;
Then, as when firſt his world its charms diſplay'd,
Beheld, approv'd, and bleſs'd the work he made.
Whether his ſong to hell's dark depth deſcend,   65
Where Night and Wo united ſway extend;
Or to fair Eden's happier climes ariſe,
Or paint the brighter ſplendors of the ſkies;

One

One boundlefs grandeur, one informing foul,
Suftains, illumes, and animates the whole.　　　70

In narrower limits, yet with epic rage,
Next view the bufkin'd mufes tread the ftage;
Where Pity o'er the wrecks of Fate reclines,
And in the dignity of Sorrow fhines;
Where Courage toils in ftorms of Fortune toft,　　75
And filent Terror ftalks in Hamlet's ghoft.
Here mighty SHAKESPEAR on his natal throne,
Unrival'd fhines, with glory all his own;
Great Nature's fav'rite, fingularly bleft,
With all the empire of the human breaft :　　　80
Him equal knowledge, equal warmth infpire,
And Wifdom tunes, and Paffion ftrikes his lyre.

In POPE's harmonious pages you may fcan,
The proper tafk and eftimate of man ;
Through various life, his various fong purfue,　　85
Which as it leads, improves in every view.
In eafy flowing numbers if he fing,
What dire effects from am'rous difcord fpring!
His pregnant fancy to our wond'ring eyes,
In various forms bids various objects rife ;　　　90
And hangs fufpended on a fingle hair,
All the conceits and whimfies of the fair.

Like grubs in amber, through his living line,
See Blackmore, Gildon, Dennis, Welfted fhine.
For when rafh witlings durft his rage inflame,　　95
He damn'd the dunces to eternal fame.

If

If led by Truth and Tafte, he trace the fcenes
Where real Beauty in full fplendor reigns,
Nature gives fanction to the critic's laws,
And fhews her fon the great fublime he draws.　　100

If nigh the filver Thames his Doric ftrain
Difplays the guiltlefs paffions of the plain,
With force united on the melting heart,
Mufic and Love their utmoft power exert.

If o'er rough rocks the torrent pours along,　　105
Thunders the roaring torrent through his fong;
If fighing breezes, wanton in the fkies,
Soft in his lay the breathing zephyr fighs.
Thus bright he fhines, in every glory crown'd,
The teft of Britifh elegance and found.　　110

But hark! what ftream of mufic pours along,
Sublimely fweet, and elegantly ftrong,
Sacred to Liberty, who rais'd his aim
To add one wreath to Cato's deathlefs fame?
'Tis ADDISON, whofe numbers court thy ear,　　115
Where Churchill's glories ever bright appear.
Thrice happy pair, with equal ardor fir'd,
By one great pow'r in one great caufe infpir'd.
Conqueft obfequious led the hero's way;
With equal fpirit glow'd the poet's lay.　　120

Verf. 118. *By one great*, &c.
　Liberty is here meant, in whofe caufe Addifon and Marlbo-
rough exerted themfelves each in their diffrent fpheres.

Who would not all the toils of war fuſtain,
To ſhine immortaliz'd in ſuch a ſtrain?
What muſe would ceaſe to ſtrike the loftieſt lyre,
Should ſuch heroic deeds their ſong inſpire?
But Wiſdom, and the Genius of mankind,   125
Another province to their ſon aſſign'd :
Britain's Spectator, in whoſe eaſy page,
At once is ſeen the gentleman and ſage.
Here Knowledge ſhines, in faireſt colours dreſs'd;
The nobleſt truths in juſteſt words expreſs'd.   130
Here cultivate your taſte, and form your ſtyle;
Here at Sir Roger's various humours ſmile;
Here view with Fancy's eyes the moral dream,
Or with new reliſh paſs from theme to theme.
Hence may you learn in every light to pleaſe,   135
To think with elegance, and write with eaſe.

With tender feeling and deſcriptive art,
Let THOMSON charm thy mind and melt thy heart.
Thomſon! enamour'd Nature's darling care,
Who bade him all her nobleſt talents ſhare ;   140
With him to ſtreams, and groves, and vales retir'd,
Inform'd his judgment, and his fancy fir'd ;
Conſign'd her faithful pencil to his hand,
And taught him all her wonders to expand :
So ſtrong his colours, ſo divine his art,   145
Such beauty forms, ſuch life inſpires each part,
With keener tranſports ſcarce our eyes purſue
The great original from which he drew.

Wouldſt thou the ardor of thy thoughts unbend,
And with the muſe to gayer themes deſcend?   150

See

See YOUNG, in quick exuberance of thought,
With all the richeft ftores of fancy fraught,
Arm Satyr's hand with darts, with fmiles her face,
And from the love of fame each action trace.

Let GARTH with fharp, but falutary fpleen,   155
As mufic gentle, but as lightning keen,
In phyfic's mock folemnity appear,
Or with correct defcription charm your ear.

The powers of Humour, Wit, and Malice join'd,
To form one bard the fcourge of human kind.   160
Sudden as plagues his mortal fhafts are thrown,
And all alike their venom'd fury own :
Not ting'd a fingle villain to difgrace,
But wound, without diftinction, all our race.
O had his rage, not men, but crimes purfu'd,   165
With milder eyes had he his nature view'd;
O'er Delicacy had not Wit prevail'd,
And in grofs pun or groffer jeft exhal'd ;
Then SWIFT in mirth and fatire might have fhown
Perfection to the world before unknown.   170

Verf. 157. *In phyfic's mock,* &c.
    In the Difpenfatory.

Verf. 158. ——— *correct defcription,* &c.
    In his Clerimont.

Spirit

Spirit and eafe wouldſt thou at once admire,
Laugh through the well-told tale with GAY and PRIOR,
PARNELL furvey, with ev'ry laurel grac'd,
HAMMOND with tendernefs, and WELSH with tafte,
The foft diftrefs of SHENSTONE's rural lay,   175
The tender plaintive dignity of GRAY,
Or he who deck'd his Lucy's urn with bays,
The foul-diffolving Orpheus of our days.

Nor muft I hear forget to recommend
BLACKLOCK — my fav'rite — intimate, and friend. 180
We from our earlieft youth to each were known,
Alike our pleafures, our affociates one:
Ah ! could I add, our kindred fouls the fame,
Both fir'd alike with one congenial flame;
Then fhould my numbers flow, like his, refin'd,   185
Delight your ear, and captivate your mind.

Thefe ornaments of nature and their age,
Shall all reward the moments they engage.

Verf. 172. ———— *Gay and Prior,* &c.

One could not forbear to include thefe two authors in fuch a lift; though, at the fame time, it muft be owned, had fome few of their tales been left out, it would have done them no dif-honour ; and one could, with more confidence, have propofed their having a place in a lady's library.

Verf. 178. *The foul-diffolving,* &c.

Lord Lyttelton. See his elegy upon Lady Lyttelton.

Thus

Thus far Direction holds her friendly light,
To animate thy tafte and guide its flight.   190
But by attentive reading now refin'd,
To its own choice fhe fafely leaves thy mind.

Yet let not verfe alone thy heart engage,
But oft revolve the juft hiftoric page.
To fancy this paft ages fhall reftore,   195
And Rome and Athens rife to view once more.
Virtue and Truth, in heighten'd colours dreft,
Embody'd here, the paffions intereft.

When ALFRED's better conftellation fhines,
When for the *fceptre* he the *crook* refigns ;   200
When WALLACE fingly, with vindictive hand,
Appears the faviour of a plunder'd land ; -
What heart can ceafe with patriot warmth to beat?
Who for their glory would not fhare their fate?

Now ftill to higher views let Reafon foar,   205
Philofophy's inchanting fcenes explore.
ASHLY humane, and NETTLETON fhall fhow,
What native joys from facred Virtue flow.

The fage whofe foul the love of Nature warms,
To trace her wonders and difplay her charms,   210
Confult attentive, and with curious eyes,
From fcene to fcene of height'ning beauty rife ;
Till all the profpect op'ning to thy fight,
Shall yield immenfe, ineffable delight ;

D   Till

Till Reafon being's end and fource fhall find,   215
And all the God-head burft upon thy mind.

Though tyrant Cuftom, with decifive air,
From Learning's calm recefs preclude the fair;
Though Pedantry, with felf-enamour'd fneer,
Pronounce domeftic toils their only fphere;   220
Their darling tenets let them ftill enjoy,
Your leifure-hours in reading ftill employ.

Yet as fociety may juftly claim
A tafk adapted to each fex and frame,
Much it imports, in active life, to know,   225
What to ourfelves, to others what we owe,
What offices from what relations rife,
And what our ftate, and what our frame implies.

Its proper place though fpeculation fhare,
Not lefs the active pow'rs demand thy care.   230
Heav'n on the foul its image has impreft,
And lighted facred Reafon in the breaft;
Yet plac'd each being in a diff'rent fphere,
And from their natures bade their tafks appear.
Domeftic duties hence alike demand   235
Th' attentive judgment, and the active hand.
Let thefe, in due degree, thy mind engage;
Nor let the woman vanifh in the fage.

O falfe to Nature, to her wifdom blind,
Who think her various tafks diftract the mind!   240

By

By thefe in one confiftent plan we rife,
Senfe makes us active, action makes us wife.
Nor refts my fong on theory alone ;
Thefe truths are likewife by experience known.
To prove the maxim juft, fhe ftill can fhow   245
A Gallic DACIER, and a Britifh ROWE.

Nor are thefe glories of the female kind
To diftant climes or periods paft confin'd.
Recent examples I might here difplay ;
But this detail till meeting I'll delay.   250
Till then, farewell, and every blefling know,
That Wifdom, Tafte, and Virtue, can beftow.

Dumfries, October 30.
1 7 5 7.

Verf. 242. *Senfe makes us active,* &c.
    Good fenfe naturally points out action as proper for beings
in our fituation : and by engaging in the active fcenes of life,
we improve in wifdom and experience.

An EVENING-WALK.

Written befide the ruins of the royal palace at Linlithgow.

By Mr R. S.

T O nations far remote the lord of day
    Now lends his chearful light; his parting beam
Yet lines with purple, and celeftial gold,
The cloud high-tow'ring from th' Atlantic deep.

From eaftern climes, how peaceful and fedate,
In fober majefty, pale Night comes on !
And o'er gay Nature's fweetly-vary'd face,
Deep-fhading all, her fable mantle throws !

Congenial Silence on her folemn fteps
Obfequious waits, and thoughtful : not a breath
Difturbs the placid air ; and on the bough
The leaf unquiv'ring hangs ; the cryftal lake
Enjoys the happy calm, nor wears a dimple
O'er all its filver furface. By her fide
Sweet Contemplation walks with penfive brow,
Intently mufing. Nature feems to feel
The foft impreffion, and finks down to reft.

Come, Genius of the Night ! come ; for the wife
Adore thy footfteps : fweet Philofophy
Hails thy approach ; for kindly thou difpell'ft

The

The noisy follies of the busy day,
And wak'st the thoughtful mind to sacred Wisdom.
Nor less the poet loves thy friendly reign,
While wand'ring forth beneath the silver moon,
Illustrious Queen! his ravish'd fancy glows,
Warm with each tender thought, each fair idea,
And all th' inchanting harmonies of song.

Now, while the busy world is laid asleep,
Inspire my soul, and brighten all her powers;
And while I wander through these solemn scenes,
Point out new beauties to the moral eye.

See there the sky, how beauteous and serene!
And there light veil'd with the gay fleecy cloud!
While here black columns of thick darkness rise,
In which perhaps ten thousand thunders sleep,
Which shall ere long their glowing prisons rend,
And shake with awful roar th'astonish'd world.

How sweetly gay is yon cerulean field,
Inlaid with all the glittering gems of heav'n,
Set by thy mighty hand, Father of light,
And love, and beauty! In the dawn of Time
Thou formedst Nature's universal frame,
Moulding its every part with sov'reign skill.
The golden sun, bright mass of vivid fire!
Thou fashion'dst in the hollow of thy hand:
Around the centre, thy omnific word,
The starry orbs in beauteous order hung,
And bade the planets know their various spheres:

Impos'd

Impos'd thofe laws by which the harmony
Of Nature is preferv'd. Then, to thy will
Obfequious, in majeftic folemn ftate,
Firft mov'd the grand machine, as by thy breath
Divine infpir'd; and ever fince has mov'd,
Inceffant trav'ling in the glorious round.

Where-e'er I caft my ravifh'd eyes abroad,
The folemn fcenes to folemn thoughts invite.
The rifing mifts, gath'ring around the hills,
Hide deep their verdant heads: o'er all the plain
The lively green finks into deepeft fhade,
And mute are all the fongfters of the day.

How fweetly awful is the pleafing gloom,
Where o'er the dewy field yon fpreading planes
Stretch wide their aged boughs! how graceful there
That beauteous fabric, once the blifsful feat
Of Caledonia's monarchs, rears its head
Aloft in air, and on the neighb'ring walls
Looks down fuperior! All-deftroying Time!
What can refift thy rage? The iron bar
Melts down before thee; and the folid rock
Moulders away. With every ftormy blaft
The fragments from yon broken arches fly.
The fpacious windows, where erewhile appear'd
Beauty and royalty, robb'd of their pride,
Are defolate and void; and in the hall,
Where once affembled fenates awful fat,
And all the pomp of majefty, there dwells
Ruin and Defolation; there the owl,

Sad favourite of Night! eludes the day;
And now, forth-iſſuing from his dark abode,
Tunes his nocturnal elegy of wo.
Yet beauteous ſtill, and lovely in decay,
The venerable ruins ſtand, and claim
A pitying ſigh from every patriot breaſt.
Here once the garden charm'd the raviſh'd eye;
Here beauteous Flora pour'd forth all her ſweets;
And here Pomona, with a lib'ral hand,
Hung with its golden load the fruitful free.

Sov'reign Director of unnumber'd worlds!
'Tis thine to bid cities and empires riſe,
And at thy pleaſure fall; to lay in duſt
The proudeſt glories of the ſons of men;
To make a deſert on the fertile plain,
And with thy beauty clothe the barren wild:
All is thy work, and all thou doſt is good.

While at this ſolemn hour the proſtrate world
Unconſcious lies, and the mad ſons of Riot
Purſue the midnight-revel, oft let me,
With all the bleſs'd tranquillity of mind
Which Innocence and Meditation give,
To ſuch delightful ſolitude repair,
And to its ſweet enthuſiaſtic joys
Give all my raviſh'd ſoul. Oft let me riſe,
On Contemplation's ever-ſoaring wing,
Above mortality, and life's low cares,
To talk with angels. Oft let Fancy ſtretch
Her boundleſs flight to regions unexplor'd;

And through ideal worlds delighted range,
Happy in her own gay creation's charms.

Blefs'd Solitude! a thoufand joys are thine;
The gen'rous, great defign; the noble thought;
The feeling heart; the boundlefs focial wifh;
The wide embrace that grafps the works of God
With univerfal love. Peaceful and calm,
With thee fair Virtue evermore remains,
And facred Wifdom makes her blefs'd abode.

Thrice lovely pair! beft ornaments of heav'n!
Your happy paths let me for ever tread,
Unweary'd follow where you point the way,
And all your footfteps rev'rently adore.

To

To SPRING.

An HYMN.

By the same.

L Ovely beauty-breathing Spring,
Waving foft thy balmy wing;
Faireft glory of the year!
On our longing plains appear.
Sweet infpirer of my fong!
On a fun-beam glide along;
Shedding round, in mingled fhowers,
Verdant herbs and fragant flowers.

See the lovely nymph appears,
And a crown of rofes wears;
Pinks and lilies mix'd are feen
On her robe of flowing green.
Welcome, welcome to thefe plains!
Welcome to the longing fwains!
Thee with ravifh'd voice I fing,
Bounteous all-reviving Spring!

Now the mornings fairer rife;
Gayer light now gilds the fkies:
Now a gentle whifp'ring gale
Softly fteals along the vale:

Now

Now the hufbandmen prepare
To improve the coming year,
Flinging free the gen'rous grain,
Hoping pleafure, bearing pain.

Living verdure clothes the hills;
Wild, along the cryftal rills,
Gillyflowers and daifies fpring,
And invite the mufe to fing.
There the fpreading bloffom fee,
Burfting forth from every tree!
Mufic wakes throughout the grove;
All is harmony and love.

Pouring forth their am'rous fong,
Hear the tuneful feather'd throng,
Perch'd on ev'ry bloomy fpray,
Swell the fweetly-dying lay!
Lowing herds, and bleating flocks,
O'er the dales and moffy rocks,
As with gladden'd hearts they range,
Speak all Nature's grateful change.

Charming Celia! come; a while
Join the univerfal fmile:
Health and Beauty breathe around
From the gay-enamel'd ground;
Smiling Nature's bounteous God
Sheds the foul of Love abroad:
Heav'n, my fair, delights to fee
Such a love as mine to thee.

See

See yon amaranthine bower,
Strew'd with many a fragrant flower!
Blooming plains, and shady groves,
Happy scenes of rural loves!
All, my love, to joy invite,
All inspire a pure delight:
Let us taste, and, tasting, sing
Every pleasure of the Spring.

✦✧✦✦✦✦✦✦✦✦✦✦✦✦✦✦✦✦✦✦✦✦✦✦✦✦✦✦✦✦✦✦✦✦✦

E P I S T L E.

To a Friend.

Written at Fort-George.

By the same.

FRom these lone walls, and this ungrateful shore,
From whence the Muses never sung before,
To thee this friendly tribute let me pay,
For thee attune the long-neglected lay.

My FRIEND!— the dear, the ever-honour'd name,
Awakes to life the near-extinguish'd flame ;
Makes every source of tenderness o'erflow,
And my fond heart with sacred transport glow.

When

When Heav'n with pity faw the fons of men
Opprefs'd with num'rous ills, and vary'd pain,
Friendfhip and Love, twin-born, celeftial pair!
He fent to lavifh all his bounties here :
For love's the beft and pureft joy we know,
The deareft blefling that we tafte below.

'Tis thine, O facred Friendfhip! to call forth
The latent feeds of unexerted worth ;
To cherifh Virtue, and to raife the mind
To nobler views, and pleafures more refin'd ;
To teach us how our follies we may cure,
Enjoy life's blefings, and its ill endure ;
To fhare our joys whene'er they overflow,
And with kind pity to divide our wo.

Take, then, for praife the wifhes of a friend ;
Heav'n mend your faults, (if you have faults to mend),
Exalt your foul ; your virtues all improve ;
The more your virtues, I the more fhall love.

Yet, fure, if aught that's good refides below,
And aught that's good 'tis granted me to know,
Honour, and Truth, and Love, and Virtue join
To make one friend; and let me call him mine!

Canft thou forget thofe dear delightful days,
When firft I fung, ambitious of thy praife ?
When, kindly-partial to the mufe you lov'd,
You urg'd her humble fong, and then approv'd ?

When,

When, with the bluſhing morn's reviving ray,
We breath'd the fragrant ſweets of orient day;
With vigour climb'd the lofty mountain's brow
Or rang'd, with jovial heart, the plain's below;
Preſs'd by her rapid foe, the tim'rous hare
Before us flying; pleaſure too ſevere!
By ſome clear ſtream, beneath the cooling ſhade,
In grateful eaſe and ſweet retirement laid,
When from his flaming throne the god of day,
Intenſely bright ſhot down his fervid ray,
We trac'd the labours of the tuneful throng,
Charm'd with the beauties of immortal ſong?

When ſober Eve, in ſable mantle clad,
Veil'd Nature's face with her delightful ſhade;
When herbs and flowers drunk up the falling dew,
And heav'n's bright queen illum'd th' ethereal blue;
When flocks were folded, and the fields were ſtill,
Save the ſweet murmurs of ſome tinkling rill;
How oft did we prolong the grateful walk,
While mutual pleaſure crown'd our ſocial talk!
When each to each might all his ſoul impart,
And ſhare th' o'erflowings of a faithful heart,
That without flatt'ry freely would commend,
Or blame with all the candour of a friend!

Did ſuch connections oft the care engage
Of this unthinking and degen'rate age,
Wiſer and better ſoon ſhould mankind grow,
And Eden flouriſh once again below.

E   Heav'n's

Heav'n's Sov'reign, powerful, wife, and gracious ftill,
Educes perfect good from partial ill:
To him I lowly bend the fuppliant knee,
And blefs the hand that fent me far from thee;
Far from the banks of Forth, the lovely plains,
Where M—— dwells, and where my foul remains.

At that dear name afrefh my forrows flow,
The copious tear, and long-indulged wo.
In all her charms fhe rifes to my view,
And all her glories fire my foul anew.
Thou amiable fweetnefs! thou fhalt long
Be the lamented fubject of my fong.
Where-e'er Heav'n's providence my ways fhall guide,
Still thy dear mem'ry fhall with me abide;
Of my fond heart be still the darling care,
The deareft, beft belov'd remembrance there.

Alas! thou other partner of my foul,
Between us mountains rife, and ocean's roll.
How oft hath Fate from me call'd thofe away
Whom of all others I have wifh'd to ftay?
How oft have I, by the fame Fate remov'd,
Languifh'd in abfence from my beft-belov'd?

Long may thy happinefs delight my ear;
Thy growing virtue let me ever hear;
Virtue alone impells to noble deeds,
And points the way that up to glory leads:
And while thou lov'ft to tread her paths divine,
So long, nor longer, let me call thee mine.

The

The POWER of WINE,

By the fame.

WIth rofes and with myrtles crown'd,
I triumph; let the glafs go round.
Jovial Bacchus, ever gay,
Come, and crown the happy day;
From my breaſt drive every care;
Baniſh forrow and defpair:
Let focial mirth, and decent joy,
This delightful hour employ.

Haſte, attend us, Wit refin'd,
Thou fweet enlivener of the mind!
And while the copious bumper's crown'd,
Bid the free jovial laugh go round.

Come, Good-nature, fhow thy face
With open fmiles and fweeteſt grace;
For ever gay: come, lovely Youth!
With honeſt Freedom, candid Truth;
Come; for without thee Mirth's a pain;
And Wit without thee flows in vain:
Chafe Melancholy far away;
Bid all be chearful, fweet, and gay.
See the fragrant rofy wine
Purpled deep with charms divine;

Shewing

Shewing, through the cryſtal glaſs,
The beauties of my lovely laſs.
For Chloe be the bumper crown'd,
While Love and Friendſhip bear it round ;
Her let every Muſe declare,
Gentle, modeſt, good and fair.

By wine the miſer generous grows ;
By wine the poet's breaſt o'erflows ;
Wine fires the warrior's ſoul with rage,
Wine gives the bloom of youth to age.
Bright wine can make the coward bold ;
Wine fills the heart with joys untold ;
Wine can tame the fierce and wild ;
Wine can make the ſavage mild ;
On us each ſocial joy beſtows,
And kindly ſoftens all our woes.

Then let's be happy while we may,
   Deſpiſing care, forgetting ſorrow ;
Enjoy the pleaſures of to-day,
   Nor fear what ills may come to-morrow.

The

The ROSE.

By the same.

FAir Rofe ! whofe lively glow the fancy warms,
Bright with a thoufand tranfitory charms;
Gay, blufhing fweetnefs; lovely, fragrant thing ;
Thy rife, thy flourifh, and thy fall, I fing.

The vernal fun now with a brighter ray,
Shed o'er the plain a more refulgent day ;
The dropping clouds their grateful fhowers diftill'd ;
The genial zephyrs warm'd the happy field,
Unlock'd earth's fertile womb, fo calling forth
The various vegetating tribes to birth ;
Now up the rigid veins, in wonted courfe,
Slowly afcends the vital fap, by force
Abforbent drawn; now here and there appear
The tender buds, and fpeak the fummer near;
And now the frefh unfolding leaves adorn,
With a gay vail of green, the fpiky thorn.

The fummer dawns, and now the potent ray
Exalts thy fweets, and calls thee forth to day ;
In fragrance rich, in lovelieft colours clad,
Thy glowing bofom to the funbeam fpread,
Charm'd we behold thee; grateful odours rife,
And on foft-fwelling gales afcend the fkies.
Beauteous all o'er the lowly fhrub is feen ;
The crimfon bloffom, and the foliage green,

E 3

Smiling with fweet diverfity appear,
The brighteft glory of the blooming year.

But ah! dear fhort-liv'd fubject of my verfe,
Why fade thy charms while I their fweets rehearfe?
Frail tranfient beauty of a fummer's day,
At once I fing thy bloom, and mourn thy quick decay.
No more thy leaves drink up the morning-dew;
No more thy bright vermilion taint we view;
No more a grateful fragrance canft thou boaft;
Ufelefs thou ly'ft, thy every glory loft.

Sweet flower! in thy decay too plain I fee
Th' inevitable fate that waits on me.
Yet fome poor minutes hence, (the powers divine
Can tell how many), and thy fate is mine.
Should lively vigour for a while remain,
Nor by pale Sicknefs hurt, nor racking Pain,
Soon fhall Old Age this healthful bloom deftroy,
And wafte with rigid hand life's every joy;
Youth's pleafing follies, Love's fweet cares be o'er,
And the once-tuneful Mufe infpire no more;
Feebler each pulfe, and fainter every breath,
Till, with victorious hand, impartial Death,
Severely kind, ftop fhort the doubtful ftrife,
And terminate the long difeafe of life.

Thou too, my Celia, dear, adored maid!
Even thou (a lovelier though the gods ne'er made)
Muft yield to cruel Time's wide-wafting rage,
And feel the preffure of invading Age.

But

But there's a beauty which can Time defy;
The beauty of the foul ean never die.
While others glory in a matchlefs face,
Too negligent of each fuperior grace,
Be God-like Virtue your peculiar care;
Virtue alone can make divinely fair.

When Beauty's charms decay, as foon they muft,
And all its glory's humbled in the duft,
The virtuous mind, beyond the rage of Time,
Shall ever bloffom in a happier clime,
Whofe never-fading joys no tongue can tell,
Where everlafting youth and beauty dwell;
Where pain and forrow never more fhall move,
But all is pleafure, harmony, and love.

✢ ✦✢✦✢✦✢✦✢✦✢✦✦✦✦✦✢✦✦✦✢✦✦✦✢✦✦✦✦✦✦ ✧✦✦✦✦✧

To N A R C I S S A.

A W A L K.

By the fame.

THE jovial feafon, and the flow'ry field,
    While Nature, in her gayeft robes attir'd,
Difplays her ev'ry glory, call us forth
To tafte the cooling fragrance of the morn.

Come

Come then, Narcissa : for thy meaneſt praiſe
‑Is to be lovely ; to be good, thy pride ;
The various beauties which indulgent Heaven
With bounteous hand hath laviſh'd on thy face,
That gentle air, that elegance of form,
And all the graces that around thee wait,
Are little to the glories of thy mind.
On that fair theme enamour'd let me dwell ;
With ſacred pleaſure mark each lovely charm,
Adoring ev'ry bright perfection there ;
Thought juſt and pure, ſenſe ſolid and refin'd,
Adorn'd with all that's lively, ſweet, and gay.
Licentious Folly hence, abaſh'd, retires,
While Chearfulneſs ſerene, and decent Joy,
For ever in Narcissa's preſence dwell.

See, my ſweet patroneſs! o'er all the eaſt
The jovial morn ſpreads out her roſy charms ;
Soon will the bright effulgent god of day
Appear in all the radiant pomp of light :
Even now the ſummit of yon verdant hill,
His welcome ray gilds with celeſtial gold ;
Advancing ſlowly to the humbler plain,
To kiſs the flowers enamour'd of his beam :
To ſee Aurora's bluſh, to tread the green,
Glitt'ring with pearly dew, to hear the voice
Of early harmony from every grove,
The fair-one's bloom not leſſens, but exalts.

In ſocial converſe, gentle, ſweet, and pure,
That lifts the ſoul to heav'n, involved deep,

Together

Together let us trace the mazy road,
Where the gay broom, and yellow blooming furze,
Profufely pour'd o'er Avon's verdant banks,
With mingling beauties glad the pleafant wild.

See where, deep-folded in their mantles green,
Yon happy groves in full luxuriance rife!
Shade above fhade magnificently gay!
Elyfian fcenes of rural joy, and peace,
And innocence; the ever-blefs'd abodes!

See yon fair eminence! whofe verdant fides
Are fring'd with woods, with herbs, and flowers adorn'd;
Its lofty head crown'd with thofe lonely walls,
Sore fhaken by the iron hand of Time;
Yet, though forfaken, ruin'd, and decay'd,
Not the leaft charm of the romantic fcene.

Quick let us pierce into the deepeft fhade,
Where-e'er the nobleft offspring of the wood,
The ftately afh, Jove's venerable oak,
The birch that fweetly fcents the ambient air,
Extended wide o'er either lofty bank,
With mingling boughs, improve the facred gloom.

Here its broad fhade the hazle-bufh difplays,
And fragrant flowers each lowly fhrub adorns
Where-e'er the void admits the folar ray;
And o'er the fummit of the rugged rock,
That bounds the channel of the murm'ring ftream,

With

With fnowy bloffoms fmiles the prickly thorn,
And fweeter than Sabean odours breathes.

Beneath the covert of th' umbrageous wood,
In fweet obfcurity fair Avon flows ;
No more inglorious, would the mufe beftow
A genius equal to NARCISSA's charms.
Perch'd on the bough projecting o'er the ftream,
Or in the centre of the grove imbower'd,
The feather'd tribes pour forth the copious fong
With artlefs melody ; the balmy air
Is full of foftnefs, harmony, and love.

Here bounteous Flora purples o'er the wild,
Scatt'ring her beauties with a lib'ral hand :
Here the wild rofe, or white or crimfon ftain'd,
Its fweetnefs breathes ; and there columbines rife,
With deep cerulean ting'd, or fnowy fair :
Gay pinks and daifies here ; the humble ftalk
On which erewhile the yellow primrofe grew.
Of herbs and flowers what multitudes befide,
By bounteous Nature's unconftrained hand
Planted, and cherifh'd by her tender care,
In fweet confufion blend their various charms ?

In confcious triumph here the goddefs reigns ·
In rude magnificence, and native glory,
Exulting, awfully retir'd fhe dwells,
And laughs at all that mimic Art can do.

Why nam'd I Nature ? Nature's fov'reign Lord

I

I meant to fing, perfection's glorious fource!
Who, felf-exiftent, from eternity,
With matchlefs wifdom laid th' illuftrious plan
Of future worlds; whofe all-creating word
Call'd them to being; whofe almighty nod
Directs their fate; whofe goodnefs infinite
Extends to all; in which they all are blefs'd.

The ferious moral ftrain NARCISSA loves;
Then look on Nature with a moral eye:
See God's own hand this fweet recefs adorn
With all the beauties that around us fmile!
He with his colours paints the blufhing rofe;
His heavenly breath perfumes the zephyr's wing,
And gives their fragrance to th' ambrofial flowers.
See in yon rock magnificent his throne!
The fong melodious from each bloomy fpray,
Is but the voice of God: the waving groves,
And all things round, the prefent God proclaim.
For though exalted high o'er ev'ry power,
In glory inacceffible he fits,
And with his thunder awes the proftrate world;
Though with his fpan he grafps immenfity,
Himfelf by none beheld or comprehended;
In all his works his bright perfections fhine;
The thoughtful mind the fair impreffion fees,
And rais'd to heav'n, loves, wonders, and adores.

Now from his flaming throne the lord of day
Pours an inceffant blaze of glory down;
Now let us feek fome peaceful cool retreat,

Where

Where the thick boughs exclude the fervid ray;
And fee! yon filvan bow'r, by Nature's hand
Form'd on the bofom of the lofty rock,
Invites our fteps. Stretching from either fide,
The mingling branches, clofe-embracing, raife
High over head a verdant canopy.
On either hand the wanton ivy forms
A fhining wall, with many a flower inlaid:
The fragrant woodbine here its fweets unfolds;
Round trees and fhrubs it twines with ftrict embrace,
And makes them gay with beauties not their own.

Down the fteep rock defcends the lucid rill,
And, gently murm'ring, pours the filver tide
In many a little cataract; below
The glaffy pool in its fair bofom fhows
The various beauties of the happy fcene.

Here might the virgin goddefs of the woods
Delight to dwell; but while NARCISSA deigns
To vifit oft with me this calm retreat,
Not all the glories which on Cynthus' brow,
Or on Eurota's banks Diana loves,
Shall this excel; nor fhail the lovely maid
Be lefs a goddefs, lefs ador'd than fhe.

To walk is pleafure and inftruction too;
Oft-times, NARCISSA, while gay Summer fpreads
Her various charms abroad, let us enjoy
Such happinefs; 'tis the beft fource of health;
And brightens all the powers of the foul;

Refines

Refines the paffions; foftens and improves
The tender feelings of the noble mind.

O let me fondly ftrive to imitate
Thy fpotlefs goodnefs, purity, and truth,
And all the virtues which thou lov'ft fo well!

With thee no forrow fhall invade my breaft;
Nor vice nor folly fhall inhabit there,
But facred innocence and pure delight.

The grateful fragrance of the breathing morn,
The fhade while glows the fierce meridian blaze,
The milder beauties of the humid eve,
With thee are full of glory, full of joy.

F   To

To CHLOE.

A SONG.

Tune, *The Birks of Invermay.*

By the same.

TO thee, my fair, the mufes fing;
   To thee the grateful tribute bring;
Kindly accept my folemn lays,
That yield inftruction more than praife.
Fair Summer, and her fmiling train,
Even now forfakes the naked plain ;
The blooming glories of the year,
No more, my Chloe, 'now appear ;
No more the lily charms the eye ;
No rofes blufh with fcarlet dye ;
They with their feafons pafs away,
Sad emblems of our own decay :
For blooming Youth muft fhortly yield,
To wafting Age, the varying field ;
Each lovely charm, each fprightly joy,
Voracious Time will foon deftroy.
Ah, mournful thought! where fhall he find
Some fweet fupporter of the mind ?
Where fhall the fov'reign balm be found,
With power to heal the bleeding wound ?

Virtue

Virtue the facred cure fupplies;
She ever lives though Beauty dies;
The lovely foul which Virtue warms
Can pleafe with everlafting charms.

Ev'n thou, ah me ! delightful maid,
And all thy beauty's charms muft fade;
But not my love, while ftill I find
A brighter glory in thy mind.
'Tis that which makes thee heav'nly fair;
That glory Time can ne'er impair :
While that continues I fhall be
Blefs'd in my love, and true to thee.

Then let us tafte, my charming Chloe,
Each pure delight, each virtuous joy;
And feize the moments kindly given,
To blefs our love, by bounteous Heav'n.
Let Innocence crown every day,
And drive each gloomy thought away :
Virtue, dear fav'rite of the fky,
Nor fcorns to live, nor fears to die.

On

On feeing a young LADY at a diſtance, and unacquainted.

By the ſame.

SEE how Saphira 'mid the croud appears!
  Around her all the loves and graces play;
Thus, o'er the lowly weeds the lily rears
  Its virgin head, with ſnowy beauty gay:
Too much, bright maid! the diſtant proſpect warms;
Then what's the preſent influence of thy charms?

So from the roſy portals of the morn,
  Cloth'd in ſweet majeſty, do we behold
The riſing ſun the happy earth adorn,
  While heaven's pure azure flames with living gold;
And from the ſplendor of his morning-rays,
We gueſs the force of his meridian blaze.

INDIF-

INDIFFERENCE.

A SONG.

Tune, *The man that's contented.*

By the fame.

A Whimfical lover's a prey to each care ;
He's loft to himfelf, while he lives to the fair ;
He dreams all the day, and he wakes all the night ;
His forrow is lafting, and fhort his delight.

The fparkling charms of the full-flowing bowl
Infpire us with friendfhip, and brighten the foul ;
Then pox on all care ! come, fill up the glafs,
And round the blythe circle, my boys, let it pafs.

Let my pretty Molly go round for the toaft ;
I'm pleas'd if fhe's mine, and the fame if fhe's loft :
As long as fhe loves me, I know fhe'll be true ;
And if fhe fhould alter — why ! fo will I too.

Should fhe be inconftant, why fhould I be fad ?
'Tis time to grow wifer, and not to go mad ;
If generous and good, fhe will value true love ;
And the lofs of a jilt is a blefling, by Jove.

The

The lofs of a miftrefs fhall never deftroy
The blifsful tranquillity which I enjoy:
Whatever may happen, I'll wifely prepare
Indifference, that fovereign cure of all care.

✤✦✤ ✤✦✤ ✤✦✤✦✤✦✤✦✤ ✤✦✤✦✤ ✤✦✤✦✤✦✤✦✤✦✤✦✤✦✤✦✤ ✤✤

To N A R C I S S A.

An E L E G Y.

By the fame.

WHile vernal airs infpire each tuneful tongue,
    Wilt thou, NARCISSA, gracioufly attend;
And while I ftrive to pleafe thee with my fong,
    With kind indulgence liften to thy friend?

If thou art pleas'd, 'tis all that I defire;
    Well fhall thy joy repay the mufe's toil;
Applauds the world, or not, I'll ne'er inquire,
    Enough to me thy fweet approving fmile.

With beauty cloth'd, again the jocund Spring
    O'er the blefs'd fields his fweeteft influence fheds;
Now fragrant odours tinge the zephyr's wing,
    And flowers unnumber'd purple o'er the meads.

In

In pride of youth exults the jovial year;
Again the groves put on their robes of green;
Again the pleafant woodland fong we hear,
And Nature in her faireft form is feen.

Along the bank of the fweet-winding ftream,
With many an herb adorn'd, and fragrant flower,
Beneath declining Phebus' foften'd beam
Oft wandering, I enjoy the fober hour.

The peaceful fcenes difpofe the tranquil breaft
To ferious mufing, and to thought refin'd;
And Contemplation comes, a heavenly gueft!
And pours out all her bleffings on the mind.

Nor when the gentle fov'reign of the night,
With her mild beam relumes th' æthereal blue,
Will I decline to hail her fober light,
As with foft fteps I print th' ambrofial dew.

Let Mem'ry then recal fome tuneful page,
And warm the foul with extafy divine;
Or let the moral thought my heart engage,
And facred Wifdom's pureft joys be mine.

Devote to Wifdom is the hour of eve;
She joys to fee the world fink down to reft;
The faithlefs paffions then no more deceive;
The cares of day no more diftract the breaft.

But

But ah! while all around is joy and peace,
Why heaves my bofom with that tender figh?
Why faints my longing heart? and why not ceafe
The tears to ftart fpontaneous from my eye?

What wants there to adorn the happy year?
And what to charm the anxious foul to reft?—
Alas! my dear NARCISSA is not here:
Tell me, ye lovers, can I then be bleft?

For thee, fweet maid! I figh and wifh in vain;
To the dear name attune the plaintive lay:
In vain does Beauty purple o'er the plain;
In vain the flowers are fweet, the groves are gay.

No more the glowing fcene my bofom warms;
No more the vernal fong delights my ear;
Thy abfence throws a vail o'er Nature's charms,
And leffens every glory of the year.

Short and uncertain is our ev'ry joy;
Oft tranfient pleafure ends in lafting wo;
Hence from the friend's, and from the lover's eye,
The luftre fades, the tears inceffant flow.

Is there a bleffing that I yet can tafte?
Let happinefs for ever wait on thee:
Be ever gracious, and be ever bleft;
Be ever kind; and Oh! remember me.

The

The L A R K S.

An E L E G Y.

Occafioned by feeing two that were fhot.

By the fame.

SUre triple brafs involv'd his cruel heart,
   Hard, and unfeeling of another's wo,
Who mark'd you victims to his impious art,
   And faw your guiltlefs blood unpity'd flow.

O'er him, while yet he in his cradle lay,
   With fond delight no happy parent hung;
Ne'er did his fmiles a mother's pain repay,
   Or gentle word drop from his lifping tongue.

His gloomy foul no fair idea charm'd;
   To him was precious wifdom never dear;
His heart the love of virtue never warm'd;
   For fuff'ring worth he never fhed a tear.

" Nor felt the tranfports of refining love,"
   Whofe facred power exalts the noble mind:
Nor friendfhip's heav'nly joys e'er did he prove;
   His fordid views to his low felf confin'd.

Unheard,

Unheard, at his inhofpitable door,
  Long might the wand'ring ftranger fhiv'ring ftand;
Perifh, for him, the needy and the poor;
  For bounty never grac'd his impious hand.

In vain his country might his aid require;
  At ev'ry vein unaided might fhe bleed:
In vain, with filver hairs, his aged fire,
  On bended knees might for compaffion plead.

For foft humanity he never knew,
  Nor focial love could in his bofom dwell,
From whofe dire hand the fatal vengeance flew,
  By which the gentle pair unpity'd fell.

No more, enliven'd by the genial fpring,
  In gay excurfions o'er the verdant plain,
Pleas'd fhall you rove, or to the morning fing,
  And with your mufic chear the village-fwain.

No more amid the pleafing green retreat,
  Sacred to love, your lowly neft prepare,
And, while affection makes each labour fweet,
  'Tend your dear offspring with unweary'd care.

Yet fhall you live while lives my humble fong;
  If not in vain your forrows I relate,
Perhaps fome gentle breaft may feel your wrongs,
  And with a tender figh lament your fate.

E L E G Y.

E L E G Y.

In the manner of TIBULLUS.

By the fame.

L ET him whofe foul the love of glory charms,
  Purchafe in fields of death immortal fame;
Be his, when worn with toil, and old in arms,
  The victor's laurel, and the honour'd name.

Me, unambitious of the noble ftrife,
  Let gentle Eafe infold with foft embrace;
Let me in calm retirement lead my life,
  Amid the joys of innocence and peace.

Let him whom gold inflames with low defire,
  The precious mifchief feek o'er land and fea:
Should he the utmoft of his wifh acquire,
  Is he more happy, more content than me?

Does Sleep with fweeter flumber feal his eyes,
  Or Fancy blefs him with more pleafant dreams?
Or does the Morn with ruddier glory rife,
  And round his head diffufe her fairer beams?

Or

Or does the radiant fov'reign of the day
 With a diviner joy infpire his breaft;
With fweeter influence drive his cares away,
 And pleas'd behold him more completely bleft?

Lay me inglorious in the lowly fhade;
 The dear delights of gentle love be mine;
With foft devotion duly fhall be paid
 My ardent vows at Cytherea's fhrine.

And fhould the gracious queen my fuit approve,
 And give my dear Narciffa to my arms;
Glory and Wealth, well are you loft for Love;
 And well repaid by Beauty's heav'nly charms.

✢✢✢✢✢✢✢✢✢✢✢✢✢✢✢ ✢✢✢✢✢✢✢ ✢✢✢✢✢✢ ✢✢✢✢✢✢✢

E L E G Y.

On the death of General WOLFE.

By the fame.

ON yonder plain what awful form appears,
 Her temples with triumphal garlands crown'd!
From her bright eyes why flow the copious tears?
 Why, fad and thoughtful, looks fhe on the ground?

'Tis

'Tis Britain's genius!—O'er her fallen fon,
   Diffolv'd in grief, the lovely mourner ftands ;
Forgets the glory by the hero won,
   And with vain fighs his precious life demands.

Low in the duft the graceful warrior lies ;
   Cold is that breaft which glow'd with martial flame ;
Eternal flumber feals his weary'd eyes ;
   No more they fparkle with the hopes of fame.

Ah ! what avails thee, number'd with the dead,
   That fair ambition which thy foul did move ?
Now life, with all its tranfient joys, is fled ;
   The charms of glory, and the fweets of love.

From Death's cold hand could valour fave the brave,
   O WOLFE ! thy country fhould not mourn thy fate ;
Could patriot virtue refcue from the grave,
   The Mufe fhould not with tears thy doom relate.

Yet 'mid the tears that wet thy facred tomb,
   Let her, well-pleas'd, in ftrains of triumph tell,
Though fnatch'd from life while in its faireft bloom,
   None ever liv'd too fhort, who dy'd fo well.

Long fhall Britannia, weeping, fpeak thy fame ;
   Thy early fate the good and brave fhall mourn,
And, ever grateful to thy honour'd name,
   Pour out their pious forrows o'er thy urn.

G   When,

When, ages hence, this fong is known no more,
  Who haply walk among the mighty dead,
Shall fay, while they thy noble fate deplore,
  And with foft fteps the hallow'd mould they tread:

" Britannia's great avenger here is laid;
  " Obfequious to his injur'd country's call,
" For her he fought, he conquer'd, and he bled;
  " Great in his life, and glorious in his fall."

✣✣✣✣✣✣✣✣✣✣✣✣✣✣✣✣✣✣✣✣✣✣✣✣✣✣✣✣✣✣✣✣✣✣✣✣

E L E G Y.

To   V E N U S.

By the fame.

G AY Venus, gentle queen of foft defire!
      Oft have I bended at thy facred fhrine;
Oft did my earneft vows of thee require
  ('Twas all I wifh'd) to call my Delia mine.

But now the dear delufion charms no more,
  I know thee deaf to my neglected pray'r;
Now ev'ry joy and ev'ry hope is o'er,
  And all behind is forrow and defpair.

Why

Why fhould I longer feek, with ufelefs care,
　　The fragrant myrtle, and fweet-blufhing rofe?
And why the garland for thy fhrine prepare,
　　Regardlefs as thou art of all my woes?

Why fhould I worfhip her who fcorns my vow,
　　And love the maid that does my love difdain?
The giver of each tender pleafure thou,
　　Yet all thou giv'ft to me is grief and pain.

The venal lover wins, with eafy art,
　　His venal fair, or bears the lofs unmov'd;
While keeneft anguifh wounds the faithful heart,
　　Or ill requited, or in vain belov'd.

Yet good and gentle is my Delia's breaft,
　　As Truth fincere, as melting Pity kind;
Not fhe, but Fate, forbids me to be bleft;——
　　To Fate true Wifdom ever is refign'd.

Farewell, ye pleafing hopes, ye fond defires;
　　Farewell, thou deareft caufe of all my pain;
Farewell, the tender fong which love infpires:
　　For life's a cheat, and love itfelf is vain.

ELEGY.

By Mr A. E.

WHen late I panted for the warlike field,
    A name in arms my firſt and great deſire,
How little did I think ſo ſoon to yield
    My heart, with glory ſmit, to Love's ſoft fire ?

But what avails the firmly-fix'd deſign,
    The moſt tenacious rule the breaſt can hold,
Since mighty Love can give the ſoul to pine,
    And melt in langour down the warrior bold ?

I'll change the ſhrill-voic'd inſtruments of death,
    No more the trumpet's ſound ſhall ſtir each vein ;
But in its ſtead the ſhepherd's pipe I'll breathe,
    And with my muſic chear the ſunny plain.

My ſturdy arms, that us'd to wield the lance,
    Henceforth ſhall only learn the crook to bear ;
I'll mingle ſportive in the rural dance,
    And for a partner ſingle out my fair.

Where doſt thou wander, fond romantic ſwain ?
    Say, has the nymph benignant heard thy pray'r ?
May ſhe not leave thee with a fix'd diſdain,
    To waſte the ſofteſt notes of love in air ?

Ah,

Ah, when my breaſt diſtends with deep-fetch'd ſighs,
  With ſweet emotion will her boſom ſwell !
Or when the tears ſtream conſtant from my eyes,
  Will kind compaſſion in the fair-one's dwell !

It muſt, it muſt ; her ſoul, to goodneſs prone,
  Will melt with pity at the tender tale :
Hence, then, ye doubting anxious cares, begone ;
  Love's genuine ſoothing voice muſt ſure prevail.

✣✣✣✣✣ ✣✣✣✣ ✣✣✣✣✣ ✣✣✣✣✣✣✣✣✣✣✣ ✣✣✣✣✣✣✣

E L E G Y.

By the ſame.

WHile other youths play ſportive in the ſhade,
    Or wanton float upon the waving ſtream ;
Beneath ſome awful tree, ſupinely laid,
  I languiſh, mourn, and of Dione dream.

The ſavage maid returns no liſt'ning ear,
  No fond endearments ſooth my ſoul to reſt :
My lengthen'd pains ſwell on from year to year,
  Nor does the proſpect bloom of being bleſt.

She little knows the heart ſhe does deſpiſe ;
  For its poor maſter's quiet too ſincere ;
How would it beat if Sorrow dimm'd her eyes,
  Or baleful Grief ſhould cauſe her ſhed a tear ?

When

When cruel Venus from the deep arofe,
   By fanning breezes o'er old Ocean roll'd,
More rapid run the ftream of human woes ;
   For then the fair firft glow'd with love of gold.

If I revolve her avaricious mind,
   The voice of reafon bids me ceafe to love ;
But let imagination paint her kind,
   Adieu the voice of reafon, can it move ?

Oft times, as, wholly loft in thought, I ftray,
   Till deep involv'd amid yon grove of pine,
Delufive Fancy there will find a way,
   To fire my breaft with hopes fhe may be mine.

Still wayward Fortune may propitious fmile,
   And blefs me with a long extent of land ;
The rifing fun may blufh upon my foil,
   And fertilize a wafte of barren fand.

The floating clouds fhall drop their fofteft rain,
   Fed by the genial fap my grafs fhall grow ;
Nutrition quick fhall fwell my waving grain,
   Before their time my laughing flow'rs fhall blow.

Then, then, my beauteous maid will bid me love ;
   My long-born pains, from that blefs'd hour, fhall ceafe ;
While wild along the gale of joy fhall move,
   The nights be tranfport all, the days be peace.

                        Where

Where was I loft? intranc'd in perfect blifs,
  The real rapture has not ftronger charms;
Almoft as happy I with dreams like this,.
  As if infolded in Dione's arms.

The vifions thefe that wave before the eyes,
  Soon as the jocund fun leads forth the morn;
Gay, vivid, tranfient, like the dew that lies,
  With tinctur'd luftre trembling on the thorn.

But now, alas! the fair delufion's o'er,.
  Reafon awakes, the gaudy vifion's paft;
Nought ftrikes my eye fave the rude rocky fhore,
  And the hoarfe wave ftill murm'ring to the blaft.

✠✠✠✠✠✠✠✠✠✠✠✠✠✠✠✠✠✠✠✠✠✠✠✠✠✠✠✠✠✠✠✠✠

E L E G Y.

By the fame.

CHerifh'd by Fortune now my work's complete,
  My bleating flocks fpread wide along the plains;
Their fleece flows graceful from Dione's feet,
  To wear the fnowy robe my charmer deigns.

Each thing has flourifh'd; on the mountain bare,
  Now waving trees fhoot out in branches wild,
Their bloffom'd fweets perfume the fluid air
  With keener odours fince Dione fmil'd.

How

How foftly do the mazy ftreamlets flow,
  With pleafing murmurs, foothing ev'n to fleep,
Did not the birds with notes, now quick, now flow,
  And fweetly-vary'd, ftill from flumb'ring keep!

Ah! who could fleep, when the melodious thrufh,
  Or lark high-foaring, fwell the long-drawn note;
While in the vacant air, or on the bufh,
  All Nature's mufic trembles from their throat?

Gods! what a change! does not each profpect pleafe,
  That lately feem'd all gloomy, and all dark?
Is not that tender heart now quite at eafe,
  That once was thought Affliction's deftin'd mark?

Tell me, ye fylvan pow'rs, what is this Love,
  That with a fmile can thus our joys inhance,
That, with a look, can ev'ry fcene improve,
  Make the heart beat, and the light fpirits dance?

Say, is it not a fympathy divine,
  That thus unites us to the graceful fair,
When fouls refin'd and gentleft minds combine,
  With faultlefs forms, and elegance of air?

Whate'er it is, I feel its fulleft pow'r,
  Dione's beauties thrill through ev'ry nerve;
The flame I'll cherifh to my lateft hour,
  Still be her flave, nor e'er from love will fwerve.

Wrote

Wrote in anſwer to a GENTLEMAN who
ſent a LADY a preſent of LANDSCAPES,
accompanied with VERSES.

By the ſame.

POets and painters ever were the ſame,
And each have felt the like congenial flame ;
Nature's the ſource from whence they've ſought applauſe ;
From her the poet writes, the painter draws.
Don't D——'s flowing lines as much diſplay
The painter's pencil, as the poet's lay ?
In the deſcriptive ſong, the waving trees,
Low bend their leaf-clad boughs before the breeze ;
The ſetting ſun before th' approach of night,
Gleams o'er the vale a yellow-ſtreaming light ;
The rocks and woods ſeen by the glimm'ring ray,
Light float before the eyes, and melt away :
In ev'ry line the rich deſcriptions glow,
The rude rock trembles, and the wild winds blow ;
Each ſtriking ſcene aſſumes a livelier hue,
The riſing flow'rs bloom fairer to the view ; .
With gaudier tints the vary'd tulips ſpring,
The dew-drops gliſter on the morning's wing :
If Niagara's cat'raċts rend the ſkies,
Swift in the verſe the foaming torrent flies,
Till in the depth below it glides along,
And ſweetly murmurs in the poet's ſong :

1

If he defcribes fome Caledonian fcene,
The tall pines flourifh in eternal green ;
Still wild and favage rife her rugged hills,
Black and difcolour'd rufh her fnow-fed rills :
But if a Scotian beauty claim his care,
His verfe is polifh'd like the blooming fair ;
The fweet attractive fmile, the mien of eafe,
The fpeaking eye, that never fails to pleafe ;
The blood that rufhes to the blufhing cheek,
And for a moment ftains the fnowy neck ;
All in the poet's words as finely fhow,
As in the living picture's mimic glow.

✦✦✦✦ ✦✦✦✦✦✦✦✦✦✦✦✦✦✦✦ ✦✦✦✦✦✦✦✦ ✦✦✦✦✦✦✦✦

L A V I N I A.

A P O E M.

By the fame.

THE fun was finking to the weftern hills,
And faintly gleam'd upon the falling rills ;
The groves were gilded with his ling'ring rays,
Whilft low-hung clouds flam'd bright with borrow'd
blaze :
Led by the beauty of the clofing day,
The loft Lavinia was feen to ftray.

Where

Where yon pure ſtream keeps daſhing o'er the rock,
And by its fall in dewy miſt is broke,
She ſtopp'd: the fond remembrance of the place
With penſive gloom o'erſpread her languid face;
While the light breeze juſt ſtirr'd the trembling leaf,
The woodland echo'd with her piercing grief.
Here let me reſt, and view this tranquil ſcene;
Ev'n here, ah me! how happy have I been;
Fair riſe the flow'rs that deck yon riv'let's ſide,
And fair I roſe, now fallen in my pride;
For in this place I loſt fair Virtue's name,
I broke all bounds, and ſacrific'd my fame:
'Twas night, I thought no human form was near,
No diſtant ſound ſtruck on my tim'rous ear,
By breathing winds the woods remain'd unſhook,
No gentle murmurs iſſu'd from the brook;
Enthuſiaſtic Fancy, fairy pow'r,
Inſpir'd me wholly in that lonely hour;
O'er all my breaſt there rag'd a piercing flame,
A fatal love for Damon tore my frame;
My boſom beat, my ſoul was all on fire,
Love ſtung each nerve, I glow'd with keen deſire;
Imagination painted out the youth,
Moulded by beauty, and adorn'd by truth:
He came, and breath'd with ſuch deluding art,
The raptures of his ſweetly-tortur'd heart,
That I by ſuch unuſual paſſions toſt,
In that ſad hour my fame and honour loſt.
'Twas happineſs a while, ſwift roll'd the time;
Abſorb'd in joy, I quite forgot my crime.

But

But now, alas! he's fled, while, all alone,
I'm left in folitary wilds to moan.
Charm'd with the glory of a martial name,
And nobly burning with a thirft for fame,
He left thofe arms, in diftant climes he roves,
Loft to Lavinia, quite forgot her loves ;
Regardlefs of the haplefs pledge I bear,
The wretched caufe of the ftill trickling tear.
Yet, yet I love him ; if I fhut my eyes,
I pray that his dear image may arife ;
One fancy'd interview can cure my rage,
Renew my tendernefs, my grief affuage.
Ye wand'ring ftreams, that murmur as ye flow !
To unknown regions bear the voice of wo ;
Oh ! bear it to the youth for whom I burn,
That may contribute to the youth's return.
And yet who knows but on fome rocky coaft,
Impell'd by driving winds, my fwain is loft ;
Naked he lies, caft on the lonely ftrand,
No foul to ftretch his corfe with pious hand ?
Or grant the ftorm o'erblows, how pafs his days ?
Through favage wilds or gloomy woods he ftrays.
Gods ! if I lofe him, whither can I fly ?
Where hide my fhame conceal'd from mortal eye !
To fome deep cave, impervious to the fun,
From keenly bitter Scorn quick let me run.
Oh, who can bear the taunting voice of Pride,
When Virtue frowns fevere, and fools deride !
Yet why defpond ? perhaps all-gracious God
Sends back the youth, and guides him on his road ;

Returns

Returns my fwain afham'd of his deceit,
By honour and by valour render'd great.
But fee the moon afcends, beneath her beam,
The trembling waters fhine with lucid gleam :
Propitious planet! dart your keeneft ray,
To light me homewards on my chearlefs way.

❧ ✦✤✦✦✦✦✦✦✦✦✦✦✦✦✦✦✦✦✦✦✦✦✦✦✦✦✦✦✦✦✦✦✦✦✦✦✦✦✦✦✦✤✦✦✦➤

Fragment of an IRISH POEM.

Taken from a literal profe tranflation.

By the fame.

SAD ! I am fad indeed, my tears ftill flow ;
Years linger on, nor fmall my caufe of wo :
Kirmor, you loft no fon, brave Conan lives ;
Daughter of Beauty, Annir ftill furvives :
Kirmr, your name blooms fair, on folid bafe;
Annyne's the laft of his unhappy race.
Autumnal winds ! blow with your fierceft breath,
And whiftle loud along yon fable heath ;
Streams of the mountains ! roar along the rock ;
Speak, tempefts ! in the proud top of the oak ;
Swift through the broken clouds, oh moon ! walk pale,
And gleam at intervals along the vale ;
Bring to my mind the fad and horrid night
(My fon, how unavailing was thy might ?)

When

When fell bold Arindil, when Daura dy'd,
When all my children fell, my greateſt pride.
As harveſt-moons thou wert, oh Daúra ! fair,
White as the ſnow before it leaves the air,
Sweet as the tender breath of broom in May,
When through our glens the calm winds ſcarcely ſtray.
Armor, in fields renown'd, with blood all ſtain'd,
Demanded her ; nor was his ſuit diſdain'd :
O'er their firm loves three happy ſhort months paſt,
Fair hop'd their friends, ſtrong wiſh'd it ſo might laſt.
Erach, the ſon of Odgal, inly pin'd,
His brother ſlain by Armor fill'd his mind;
Like the ſea's ſon he came ; on the bold wave
Fair was his ſkiff, fair was the ſhew it gave ;
White were his locks of age, rude was their flow,
And calmly thoughtful was his ſerious brow.
" Faireſt of women, Daura ! in the ſea,
" A rock not diſtant bears a waving tree ;
" Its branches are extended wide in air,
" And from afar the wild fruit bluſhes fair :
" There Armor waits ; come, Daura, ſwiftly move ;
" For me he ſent to fetch his beauteous love."
She went ; for Armor call'd : Armor ! ſhe cry'd ;
Save the rock's ſon no other voice reply'd !
Armor ! my love, torment me not with fear ;
'Tis Daura calls ; hear, ſon of Ardnart, hear.
Fleet o'er the rolling tide the traitor fled,
With ſmiles deriding the deluded maid.
My father ! brother ! Armor ! help ! oh hear !
She mournful cry'd ; it mournful reach'd the ear.

My

My fon defcended from the hill's fteep face,
All rough and manly in the fpoils o'th' chace;
His trufty bow was grafp'd within his hand,
Five dogs purfu'd his fteps along the ftrand;
He faw fierce Erach, and he feiz'd him bold,
A hide's thick thongs around his limbs are roll'd,
Bound to an aged oak he loudly moans,
He loads the winds with unavailing groans.
Swift in his boat my fon divides the deep,
'Twas Daura call'd, Daura was heard to weep.
The furious Armor from the beach difmifs'd,.
The feather'd fhaft, along the air it hifs'd,
And finking deep, no more his heart was fir'd;
He fell, and as he reach'd the rock, expir'd.
My fon! my Arindil! you timelefs fell,
And in the traitor's place I live to tell.
Armor plung'd in, refolv'd to fave the fair;
He lafh'd the flood, his brawny limbs all bare;
Mounting the furgy wave, he left the fhore,
A blaft o'erwhelm'd him, and he rofe no more!
Alone, and on the fea-beat rock, my child
Was heard complaining, all her accents wild,
Oh, loud and frequent were her pitious cries!
Nor could her father's feeble aid fuffice:
All night her mournful wailings reach'd my ear,
All night I harrow'd was with dread and fear;
Loud was the wind, and on the mountain's fide,
Hard beat the rain, hard beat the foaming tide:
I heard at laft her trembling voice decay,
As winds i'th' mountain-grafs, it dy'd away!

O'ercome

O'ercome with grief, my Daura breath'd her laft;
Thee Armyne left with clouds of wo o'ercaft.
When come the mountain-ftorms, when tempefts fly,
When the fierce north-wind lifts the wave on high,
I fadly fit upon the founding fhore,
I view the rock, and hear the fea's wild roar;
The direful profpect feeds my troubled foul,
Still gufh my tears, ftill fierce my eye-balls roll.
Oft by the fetting moon I fee the dead;
Pale rife their ghofts, I think I hear their tread;
Half viewlefs they together feem to walk,
They feem in mournful conference to talk;
Will none of you this ftubborn filence break?
In pity to a drooping father, fpeak.

Sad! I am fad indeed, my tears ftill flow;
Years linger on, nor fmall my caufe of wo.

The

The STARLING, the CROWS, the FOX,
and the HAWK.

A FABLE.

By the fame.

A Starling long had rang'd the woods,
And long had skimm'd the waving floods;
A master in diffimulation;
For lying was his inclination:
No fawning minister of state,
Could ever match him in deceit.
He happen'd once his way to wing,
When bounteous Nature sends the Spring,
To swell, with vary'd sun and show'rs,
The early blooms and tender flow'rs;
Nigh where a grove of trees arose,
He lighted by a troop of crows,
And thus with specious lying words,
He strait address'd the sable birds:
For shame, my friends, what seek ye here,
When glorious carrion is so near?
This very morn the murd'rous knife,
Depriv'd an aged horse of life:
I saw the butchers plunge it in,
While tanners stripp'd him of his skin:
You'll find him near that rising hill,
Away, away, and eat your fill.

He ended: Off at once they fly,
Their pinions cleave the yielding fky.
Old wily Reynard next he meets,
Whom thus with fhew of love he greets:
Your humble fervant, mafter Fox,
I've often heard your fond of cocks;
You grin, I fee, and ftrive to blufh,
Obferve yon barn; but, hark ye, hufh!
All in the funfhine of the day,
Two gamefome young ones fport and play.
Sly Reynard made a bow and leer,
Then fcamper'd to his fancy'd cheer:
The felf-approving bird arofe,
With fuch fuccefs his bofom glows;
When lo a hawk of monftrous fize,
Comes fweeping down the azure fkies,
The trembling Starling bleeds, and dies.

Thus fares it with the modifh youth
Who tells you ev'ry thing, but truth;
And ftrict Veracity defying,
Humbuggs, a modern word for lying;
Credulity pricks up his ears,
And with a fix'd attention hears;
Ten thoufand Frenchmen newly flain,
Lie breathlefs fmoaking on the plain;
Our fleets too met upon the feas,
And ours has beat the French with eafe;
Away they ran to fave their bacon,
Yet half a dozen fhips are taken.

The wretch too banishes each tie
Of nature and humanity,
Delights to fee the virgin's tears,
When for her lover's death she fears;
He thinks there's mufic in the groans
Of mothers weeping for their fons:
But foon as once he is detected,
Each thing he utters is fufpected;
Each thinking mortal will defpife
The man who glories in his lies.
Forbear the bafe unmanly guile,
Ah! wound not others for a fmile;
Think on the forrows that you raife,
Embitter not the virgin's days.
Say, can you hear unmov'd, her figh?
Or joy to fee her tear-ftain'd eye?
Believe me, fuch a wicked part
Denotes a mean and tainted heart:
However, if you needs muft lie,
Avoid the next fin, perjury;
There 'tis advifeable to ftop;
The cure's a pillory or rope.

A

A PASTORAL BALLAD.

In the manner of SHENSTONE.

By the fame.

I.

HOW could you deceive me, my fair ?'
　　How tell me you opennefs lov'd ?
How perfuade me my fad penfive air
　　Was by you not difdain'd, but approv'd ?
And yet the delufion had pow'r
　　For to charm my whole fenfes away ;
I gaz'd on you hour after hour,
　　And to pleafe fram'd the rude rural lay.

II.

While my foul was all melted in love,
　　While each nerve and each pulfe wildly beat,
You a paffion as ftrong feem'd to move ;
　　Who e'er could have dream'd 'twas deceit ?
When I fault'ring attempted to fpeak,
　　My confufion was cur'd with a fmile,
You ftrove my fond filence to break ;
　　Yet this was all meant to beguile.

III.

III.

How oft have we carelesly ftray'd,
　While the moon feebly lighted the vale,
And under the cool ev'ning fhade,
　Prolong'd the foft amorous tale?
Then the wind could not fhake the light leaf,
　Nor the river roll loudly along,
Nor the nightingale breathe out her grief,
　But you fearfully clafp'd me more ftrong.

IV.

Thofe days are ftill frefh in my view,
　When I fearch'd where the violet blows,
And tore from the fpot where it grew,
　The briar, or wild-fpreading rofe:
You was pleas'd with the trifles I cull'd,
　And urg'd to repeat the fond tafk,
And ftill, though I frequently pull'd,
　You, frequent delighted, would afk.

V.

Now far other tranfports are mine,
　Far other employments I find ;
No more I your garland entwine,
　You oft have refus'd it, unkind :
Each moment I pour forth my fears,
　Tales of wo to the woods I impart,
Which, though oft interrupted by tears,
　Yet mournfully footh my fad heart.

VI.

VI.

Now I fee that Unfaithfulnefs reigns,
  That a fond conftant nymph is a dream ;
Deceit is found roving the plains,
  And winding along ev'ry ftream :
Of the change, ah, ye fhepherds, beware,
  Nor truft the allurements of art ;
Believe not the falfe fmiling air,
  Since the tongue's not allied to the heart!

VII.

Farewell to the flocks I have fed !
  Farewell to the flow'rs I have rear'd !
Farewell to the fweet-breathing mead,
  Where fo often with you I've appear'd !
I fly, yet I love you, my fair ;
  Perhaps you'll repent when I'm gone ;
My bofom fhall nourifh defpair,
  And I'll figh that all pleafure is flown.

S O N G.

S O N G.

By the same.

I.

HOW blefs'd is the man who fupplies
Each day and each hour with new charms,
Whofe heart, foon as one paffion dies,
Another as fierce ftill alarms?
He never is troubled with care,
No vexation to him are his loves;
For he flies, or remains with the fair,
As his fuit fhe neglects or approves.

II.

But I, a poor conftant weak fwain,
Whofe heart is immoveably fix'd,
Although I'm repaid with difdain,
And my days are with pleafure unmix'd,
Still faithful am found to one fair,
Still fervilely hang at her feet,
Still vainly prefer my fond pray'r,
Though fure a refufal to meet.

III.

How pleafing it is to explore,
Each country and kingdom remote,
Survey all the charms of each fhore,
And the beauties of ev'ry fweet fpot!

How

How ignoble to breathe out one's days,
On our own native bit of dull ground,
Perfevere in the fame ftupid ways,
And walk in the fame tirefome round!

✠✠✠✠✠✠✠✠✠✠✠✠✠✠✠✠✠✠✠✠✠✠✠✠✠✠✠✠✠✠✠✠✠✠✠

An E L E G Y.

Occafioned by the death of Mrs ✻ ✻ ✻ ✻ ✻

By Mr BEATTIE.

STill fhall unthinking man fubftantial deem
The forms that fleet through life's deceitful dream?
On clouds, where Fancy's beam amufive plays,
Shall heedlefs Hope his tow'ring fabric raife;
Till at Death's touch the fairy vifions fly,
And real fcenes rufh difmal on the eye,
And from elyfium's foothing flumbers torn,
The ftartled foul awakes, to think — and mourn!

O ye whofe hours in jocund train advance,
To Joy's foft voice whofe fprightly fpirits dance,
Who flow'ry fcenes in endlefs view furvey,
Glitt'ring in beams of vifionary day!
Oh! yet while Fate delays th' impending wo,
Be rous'd to thought, anticipate the blow;

Left,

Left, like the light'ning's glance, the sudden ill
Flash to confound, and penetrate to kill;
Left, thus involv'd in deep funereal gloom,
With me you bend o'er some untimely tomb,
Pour your wild ravings in Night's frighted ear,
And half pronounce Heaven's sacred doom severe.

Wife! beauteous! good! —— Oh! every grace com-
    bin'd
That charms the eye, that captivates the mind!
Fair —— as the flower just opening to the view,
Whose leaves the Morning bathes in pearly dew!
Sweet —— as the downy-pinion'd gale, that roves
Fraught with the fragrance of Arabian groves!
Mild —— as the strains, that, at the close of day
Warbling remote, along the vales decay! ——
Yet, why with these compar'd? What tints so fine,
What sweetnefs, mildnefs, can be match'd with thine?
Why roam abroad, since still to Fancy's eyes
I see, I see the lov'd idea rise?
Still let me gaze, and every care beguile,
Gaze on that cheek where all the graces smile;
That foul-exprefling eye, whence, mildly bright,
Fair Goodnefs beams on the transported sight;
That polish'd brow, where Wisdom sits serene,
Each feature forms, and dignifies the mien.
Still let me listen, while her words impart
Delight deep-thrilling through the glowing heart;
And all the foul, each tumult charm'd away,
Yields, gently led, to Virtue's easy sway.

         Adorn'd

Adorn'd by thee, bright Virtue, Age is young,
And mufic warbles from the falt'ring tongue ;
Thy ray creative chears the clouded brow,
Touches the faded cheek with rofy glow,
Illumes the joylefs afpect, and fupplies
A lively luftre to the languid eyes;
Each look, each accent, while it awes, invites,
And Age with every youthful grace delights.
But when Youth's bloom reflects thy bright'ning beams,
On the rapt view the blaze refiftlefs ftreams;
Th' ecftatic breaft triumphant Virtue warms,
And Beauty dazzles with angelic charms.
Ah! whither fled ! ——ye dear illufions ftay ! ——
Lo! pale and filent lies the lovely clay !
How are the rofes on that lip decay'd,
Which Health fo late in vivid bloom array'd !
Health on her form each fprightly grac'd beftow'd,
With active life e '. fpeaking feature glow'd.
Fair was the flower, and foft the vernal fky ;
Elate with hope we deem'd no tempeft nigh ;
When lo! a whirlwind's inftantaneous guft
Laid all its beauties withering in the duft.

All cold the hand that footh'd Wo's weary head !
All quench'd the eye the pitying tear that fhade !
All mute the voice, whofe pleafing accents ftole,
Infufing balm, into the rankled foul !——
O Death ! why arm with cruelty thy power !
Why fpare the weed, to lop the fragrant flower !

Why

Why fly thy shafts in lawlefs error driv'n!
Is Virtue then no more the care of Heav'n!
But peace, bold thought! be ftill, my burfting heart!
We, not ELIZA, felt the fateful dart.
Scap'd the dark dungeon dees the flave complain,
Nor blefs the hand that broke the galling chain!
Say, pines not Virtue for the lingering morn,
Doom'd on this midnight-wafte to ftray forlorn!
Where Reafon's meteor-rays, with fickly glow,
O'er the dun gloom a dreadful glimmering throw,
Difclofing dubious to th' affrighted eye
O'erwhelming mountains tottering from on high,
Black billowy feas by endlefs tempefts tofs'd,
And weary ways in wildering lab'rinths loft.
Oh! happy ftroke, that breaks the bonds of clay,
Darts through the burfting gloom the blaze of day,
And wings the foul with boundlefs flight to foar
Where dangers threat, and fears alarm, no more!

Tranfporting thought! here let me wipe away
The falling tear, and wake a bolder lay——
But ah! afrefh the fwimming eye o'erflows——
Nor check the tear that ftreams for human woes——
Lo! o'er her duft, in fpeechlefs anguifh, bend
The hopelefs PARENT, HUSBAND, BROTHER,
    FRIEND!
Vain hope of mortal man!——But ceafe thy ftrain,
Nor Sorrow's dread folemnity profane;
Mix'd with yon drooping mourners, o'er her bier,
In filence fhed the fympathetic tear.

From the Italian of T A S S O.

A H me! vile intereſt every boſom ſtains,
　　　From mighty monarchs, down to ſimple ſwains:
No more alas! to palaces confin'd,
But reigns unbounded in the peaſant's mind;
Be then this age, pronounc'd the *Age of gold*,
Since even happineſs for pelf is ſold.
But thou, ignoble wretch, who firſt eſſay'd
To charm, by ſordid arts, the venal maid;
Taught the young breaſt on hopes of gain to rove,
(Fair faith neglected and unſpotted love) ;
Eternal curſes blaſt thy hated name,
Thou bane of life, of human kind the ſhame.
For thee, no friend a monument ſhall rear,
For thee, ne'er heave the ſigh, ne'er drop the tear;
To ſoothe thy ghoſt, ne'er ſhall the lyre be ſtrung,
Ne'er ſhall thy name diſgrace the poet's ſong ;
When to the turf, where thy pale reliques lie,
Some neighb'ring ſwains ſhall guide the wand'ring eye,
Inform the traveller what vile remains,
What hated duſt th' unhallowed ſpot contains ;
No honours to thy mem'ry ſhall he pay,
Nor peaceful *requiem* for thy *manes* ſay.

Nipt by the blaſts of peſtilential air,
Ne'er may the rural verdure flouriſh there,

But

But horrid Winter ſtretch its dread domain,
And ſtorms eternal deſolate the plain.
'Twas Avarice firſt inverted Nature's plan,
And chang'd the happineſs deſign'd for man;
Meanly corrupted love's ſublimer fires,
And fully'd all the joys of ſoft deſires:
But mankind ſtill with horror ſhall behold,
The maid who proſtitutes her heart for gold.

✤✤✝✤✤✝✤✝✤✤✝✤✤✝✤✤✝✤✤✝✤✤✝ ✝✤✝✤✤✝✤✝✝ ✤✤✝✤✝✤✝✤✝✤✝✤✝✤✝✤ ✤

From the Italian of G U A R I N I.

D Ear happy groves! where peace eternal reigns,
And ſolemn ſtillneſs overſpreads the plains;
Once more, ſweet vale! thy beauties I ſurvey,
Hail thy hoar ſhades, and negligently ſtray
Where chance directs, or fancy points the way.
Here let me reſt!——and oh! my fate incline,
To fix this humble habitation mine;
Where genuine happineſs, long ſought, I find,
And calm repoſe, well ſuited to my mind.

Deluded mortals! who ſo vainly prize
Fantaſtic joys, yet ſolid bliſs deſpiſe;
Poſſeſs'd of opulence, poſſeſs'd of power,
Indulge and ſtill indulge the wiſh for more:

For

For what avails an old illuftrious line,
Or what the bloom of youth, or form divine?
What though the joyous dance, and feftal fong,
Pour their full tide of happinefs along?
With cluft'ring vineyards, fertile fields confpire,
To crown each wifh, and fatiate each defire?
If difcompos'd the wayward paffions roll,
And fair Content is banifh'd from the foul?

What happinefs attends the rural maid,
In native charms and artlefs drefs array'd;
Alike unconfcious of the ills that wait
On Fortune's fmiles or Poverty's low ftate!
Poor but content: to grandeur though unknown,
Yet freedom, health, and peace, are all her own:
Her drink the pure tranflucent fountain yields,
And health fhe gathers from the teeming fields;
Nor vainly for a coftly mirror fighs,
While the fame cryftal ftream the want fupplies.
Thus far remov'd from all that vex the great,
The glare of courts, and infolence of ftate;
Where War's rude trump ne'er founds its dire alarms,
Nor calls the peaceful cottager to arms;
From noife and tumult free, and void of fear,
All on the plain, fhe tends her fleecy care.
Haply for her fome fwain tranfported burns,
And fhe with equal warmth his flame returns:
Blooms her fair form? It blooms for him alone,
Whom love, untaught to feign, has made her own;

While

While fhe the dictates of her heart avows,
Nor jealoufy fufpects, nor violated vows.
Together thus, in calm fequefter'd bow'rs,
They while away the pleafurable hours;
Their paffions, fixt and conftant, glow the fame,
Nor aught, but death, extinguifhes the flame.

+·+·+ +·+·+·+·+·+·+·+·+·+ +·+·+·+·+ +·+·+·+·+·+·+·+·+·+·+·+·+·+·+·+

E P I T A P H.

On a Young Lady.

IF worth departed claims the heart-felt tear,
Oh ftop! and let it ftream profufely here,
Where humbly lies what once had ev'ry art,
To warm, to win, to captivate the heart;
A foul to tendernefs and foftnefs prone,
That kindly mourn'd for forrows not its own,
Yet, firm and refolute, did well fuftain
Acuteft anguifh, and terrific pain:
Hence the fad fource of thy lamented doom,
Hence immaturely hurried to thy tomb.

Yet why complain, or why thy fate deplore,
Since thefe fierce pangs diftrefs thy form no more?
Or why reluctantly thy life refign,
Since now unmingled happinefs is thine?

Yet

Yet will thy gentle fhade forgive the tear
That fprings from honeft grief, and love fincere;
Forgive the friend that tunes thefe plaintive lays,
Sacred to thee and thy lov'd virtues praife :
Thefe all the honours we can now beftow,
And thefe alone the foft'ners of our wo.

✚✚✚✚✚✚✚✚✚✚✚✚✚✚✚✚✚✚✚✚✚✚✚✚✚✚✚✚✚✚

E P I T A P H.

THongh no proud trophies of the great, or vain,
  No vaunts of anceftry, no venal ftrain,
Bedeck this humble monument: yet here,
Unbought, unafk'd, fhall ftream the grateful tear;
Here fhall the orphan mourn its parent gone;
Here the lorn widow pour th' unceafing moan;
Here Virtue's friends their tribute oft fhall pay,
Recall his various worth, and fighing fay,
" Oh ! he was mild, benevolent, humane;
" Though gentle, firm; though delicate, not vain;
" Fond to fcorn'd worth his gen'rous aid to lend;
" The poor man's guardian, and the good man's friend;
" Poffefs'd of patience, when feverely try'd;
" The Stoic's fortitude, without his pride;
" Whofe nobler foul difdain'd the farce of fhow;
" Who liv'd unblemifh'd, and who left no foe."

Though

Though now from hence by Heav'n's high will remov'd,
Yet be his mem'ry honour'd ftill, and lov'd;
While from this tomb each mourner fhall depart,
With mended morals, and a purer heart.

✢✢✢✢✢✢✢✢✢✢✢✢✢✢✢✢✢✢✢✢✢✢✢✢✢✢✢✢✢✢

E P I T A P H.

For the Rt Hon.

MARY Countefs of ERROL.

SOft! paffenger! the moral lay attend,
And life's folicitudes a while fufpend;
Survey this tomb, with no regardlefs eye,
And mark the place where ERROL's afhes lie;
In whom her great anceftors merits fhone,
Though foften'd, and embellifh'd by her own:
Blefs'd with each virtue that deferves applaufe;
The form auguft, that veneration draws;
The clear difcerning head; the foul ferene,
Calm, and compos'd, through life's perplexing fcene;
Reafon's ftrong force; Religion's purer flame,
That mildly glow'd, ftill genuine, ftill the fame;
Averfe to all the fplendid toils of ftate,
In private happy, and unenvy'd great;

Whofe

Whofe heart, not harden'd to the wretch's moan,
Felt all his anguifh, and forgot its own;
Nor only felt, but with attentive care,
Reprefs'd the figh, and wip'd the ftreaming tear;
While Patience, beaming all its lenient rays,
Benignly deck'd the evening of her days,
And taught her foul, fuperior ftill and wife,
To view approaching death with placid eyes;
At length —— with brow ferenc, and paffions ev'n,
She gently breath'd her guiltlefs foul to heav'n.

✦✛✜✦✦✛✦✛✛✦✛✦✛✛ ✛✦✛✦✛✦✛✛✦✛ ✦ ✛✦✛✦✛✦✛✦✛ ✛✛

TRANSLATION of an epiftle of the *Oeuvres du Philofophe de Sans-Souci:*

A collection of poems (lately publifhed) wrote by the King of Pruffia.

E Φ I S T L E XIX.

From the King of PRUSSIA *to his Private Secretary Monf.* DARGET.

PAtient tranfcriber of my painful ftrain,
Guardian of all the labours of my brain;
Tell me, Darget, from ceremony free,
What think you of a mafter form'd like me?
From long-protracted folitude, become
Abfent, unequal, melancholy, dumb.

Who,

Who, for whole days, fits plodding o'er a book,
No algebraift with a fourer look,
Slighting each joy that Pleafure would impart,
Thought on his brow, and forrow at his heart.
Speak out, Darget, to reafon canft thou bring
A life fo mortify'd in fuch a king ?

 A king, ye gods! methinks I hear thee cry,
While the big wifh fits fparkling on thine eye,
" Would gracious Heav'n indulge me with a crown,
The gods themfelves fhould look with envy down;
No crabbed problem fhould my thoughts purfue,
But beauty, ever kind as well as new :
Would fome well-judging people make me king,
From morn till night I'd drink, and dance, and fing;
Search all them agazine of things below;
Is there a blifs forbidden kings to know ?
Where-e'er their moft fantaftic wifhes fall,
Some ready flave anticipates the call;
Kings can condemn, or pardon, fave, or kill,
And make it peace, or give us wars at will;
Idols of earth, and fav'rites of the fkies,
'Tis theirs to tafte new pleafures as they rife.
Hail, happy ftate of demigods below,
Where unimbitter'd pleafures ever flow :
Hail, happy ftate of tranfport, and of reft,
Where none but fools, or madmen, are unbleft."

 Soft, good Darget, let paffion ne'er prevail,
But cool inquiry hold the pond'ring fcale :
          Let's

Let's view thofe pleafures with impartial eyes,
And coolly trace the fubject as it lies.

Fortune for thee has humbly drefs'd the fcene,
Metting thy pleafures with her golden mean.
Mediocrity prefents the well-mix'd bowl,
To opiate every forrow of thy foul;
Not niggard quite, nor lavifh of her ftore,
Has giv'n thee juft enough, and nothing more.
What greater curfe can Providence decree
Than indigence, or fuperfluity?
Extremes are but the wayward tricks of Nature,
Or dwarf or giant, 'tis a monftrous creature;
Ill drefs'd alike the beggar and the beau,
Who fhrinks in rags, or fweats in ermin'd fhew:
Soft Peace for thee forfakes the kingly crown,
To wrap thy temples in her nightly down;
While blefs'd, without folicitude, or forrow,
Thy tafte of prefent blifs excludes to-morrow.

Too happy man, from ev'ry danger free,
That overwhelms the great, and preffeth me;
Too mean for envy, too obfcure for foes,
The ftorms of cenfure lull thee to repofe.

If when at home thy praife-deferving wife,
Forbears to ftun thee with domeftic ftrife,
At eve returning with fatigue opprefs'd,
If fhe receive thee fondly to her breaft;

If

If no collected rheums invade thine eyes,
If Dalichamp * with proper health supplies;
What other blifs has Providence in ftore?
Darget, miftaken mortal, afk no more.

Yet, as I fpeak, methinks I hear thee call
My prudent counfel, declamation all.
Talk ne'er fo wife, and reafon as I will,
That frigid face looks oppofition ftill ;
Condemns my fine defcription as untrue,
And far more bright than nature ever drew.

Well then, we grant that Heav'n fome pain difpenfes,
In making thee a king's amanuenfis,
Who oft for hours purfues the fcribbling fit,
And, mercy on us! takes it all for wit ;
Who fancies ready Fame prepares to hear,
And echo back his trafh in ev'ry ear:
Then when the live-long page is copied out,
Makes, Heav'n defend our hearing! fuch a rout ;
On ftops and points exhaufts his indignation ;
A comma here has quite miflook its ftation ;
And here a dafh —— and there a blank   fhould be,
Hyphen! parenthefis! apoftrophe!
That fatal period fets the fenfe at odds,
All muft be copied fair, by all the gods.
Thus damn'd once more to drefs the page divine,
You wifh him at the devil every line.

* A furgeon.

K   It

If fuch the faithful portrait of thy woes,
If fuch the fource whence ev'ry forrow flows,
Come on, my friend, and let us calmly try,
Who beft deferves compaffion, you or I ;
Try what eftate can beft from forrow fave,
And wifely weigh the monarch with the flave.

Yet, think I not intend to deck my rhimes
With paradox, the blufh of modern times ;
Or fmoothing falfehood with ingenious care,
Give fome exploded trafh a novel air.
The truths I tell, I feel them at my heart,
Truths which even pride forbids me to impart.

Severe the tafk, and rigid is the fchool,
And harder than all arts, the art to rule :
The king, who winds through each detail of ftate,
Who ftudies to be good, as well as great;
Who fills th' incumbent duties of his reign,
Can only boaft pre-eminence of pain.

On either fide impofing equal laws;
Fixing determin'd dates to every caufe ;
If Juftice over Difcord would prevail,
And refolutely fix the wav'ring fcale,
Behold a fiend that keeps the world in awe,
Chicane, with all her hundred dogs of law ;
Forth iffuing furious from her dark abode,
Spurns with contempt the legiflative code.

But,

But, ftranger ftill ! even thofe who difagree,
Receive, diffatisfy'd, the quick decree,
And with a fund of long debate fupply'd,
Judge from caprice the juftice of their fide.

Impofing taxes next require his fkill ;
Where each contributes fore againft his will.
Ambition's wifh, the courtier's lacker'd pride,
Is by the grudging cottager fupply'd.
Whence each their different difcontents exprefs,
One afks for more, and t'other would give lefs.
To ev'ry tax while that avows diffenfion,
From ev'ry tax this hopes a nobler penfion.
Each loud exclaims at each, yet all agree,
To arrogate redrefs from majefty.
Happy the king in lore hermetic fchool'd,
Could he content them both by making gold :
Yet happier, far more happy, could his laws
Reftore the commonwealth which Plato draws.

The hardy foldier next demands his care,
And rigid difcipline with brow fevere ;
The furious warrior, eager for debate,
If unemploy'd, would overturn the ftate.
By their prætorian bands, the Romans faw
A venal empire, and fubverted law.
Lions of war, impatient to command,
Themis muft rule them with her iron hand.
Yet not feverity alone will do,
But threats, and hopes, and fometimes flatt'ry too :

Their

Their force together muſt united run,
And all the hundred thouſand act as one ;
Compact the vaſt machine muſt learn to roll,
A king, the central nave, that moves the whole :
This to effect requires unbounded care,
The half too much for one alone to bear.

" Well then, at laſt, the catalogue is done."
Patience, my friend, 'tis ſcarcely yet begun.
Cares follow care, and toils ſucceed to pain,
I've ſhew'd a few, but hundreds yet remain.

The rights of kingdoms next his peace aſſail,
His policy muſt guide the public weal :
To rivals, friends, his conduct muſt oppoſe,
And theſe demand reſtraint, and ſuccour thoſe.
Thus ba'anc'd each European pow'r is free,
All finding in diſtruſt, ſecurity.
If kings were juſt, and treaties were ſincere,
Small were the taſk, and light the ſtateſman's care.
But when contracting powers, by int'reſt ſway'd,
Make politics a low deceiving trade ;
When fraud, of caution, falſely bears the name,
And turns to ſcience what ſhould make our ſhame ;
When truth appears no more, but every ſtate
Abounds with men, whom crimes have render'd great ;
Even Wiſdom's ſelf muſt learn to change her ſide,
And combat crimes with arms by crime ſupply'd.
Treaties with two-fold meaning well deſign'd,
Muſt ſeem to faſten, and yet nothing bind..

Conventions

Conventions firm as zephyrs when they blow,
Muſt be prepar'd, and copied out for ſhow :
Hence genuine virtue no delight can bring,
Since crimes themſelves are virtues in a king.

Few are the friends an hapleſs monarch knows,
His neareſt neighbours are his greateſt foes.
While theſe ambitious views in ſecret frame,
'Tis his to counteract each fav'rite ſcheme ;
And pond'ring how their words and acts agree,
Read in the preſent, dark futurity.
Thus, wherefoc'er he turns, whate'er he tries,
Dangers unſeen, and diſappointments riſe.
As when beſiegers, anxious for renown,
Advancing o'er the glacis of a town,
With cautious ſteps, and ſlow, explore around,
Nor truſt their ſafety to the hollow ground,
Where many a death in boſom'd ambuſh lies,
And thunders long to meet their kindred ſkies ;
Such is the ſkill, and ſuch the caution ſhown,
In diſappointing mines that ſap the throne.

But grant each duty done, alas ! in vain :
His thoughtleſs, thankleſs ſubjects, ſtill complain :
In ev'ry ſcience thoſe expect him ſkill'd,
In commerce, laws, in council, and the field.
Thoſe who are puniſh'd, blame his harſh decree;
The proſecutors blame his lenity.
Is he for war ? From hence freſh clamours ſpring,
" Heav'ns ! what a curſe, ambition in a king!"

K 3

Is

Is he for peace? " Our prince, in idiot ſtate,
" Fears the loud call that animates the great.'ᵗ
Rules he alone? his caution each accuſes,
Who counſel wiſer than his own refuſes.
Does he permit his miniſters to rule?
Then each perceives the monarch but a tool.
Has he a fav'rite? all his weakneſs ſee:
Without, 'tis mere infenſibility.
If free, defpis'd; if ceremonious, nice;
But gallantry compriſes ev'ry vice.
Vain, very vain, my friend, are all who can
Hope for perfection in imperfect man;
Their crowns, aud globes, and thrones, and ointments too,
Lift kings not one inch nearer heav'n than you.
To fix a faultleſs monarch on the throne,
Let ſculptor Adam carve him out in ſtone;
For none but ſuch can 'ſcape each envious blow,
Which Cæſar felt, and Titus learn'd to know.

Aſk you, why Obloquy with angry frown,
Still glances at the head that wears the crown!
The anſwer's plain: for ſome, by nature free,
Deteſt whatever checks their liberty.
Others again, with ſmaller cauſe of hate,
Envy the glitt'ring tinſel of his ſtate.
One to his friend in ſecret ſeems to cry,
" Ah! could our monarch learn to think as I."
Another openly: " Were I in his place,
Things ſhould put on a very different face."

See,

See, to repair their ſhatter'd fortunes ſome,
With ſmiles and bows, and long petitions, come ;
Tell me, Darget, can ſuch a king as I,
Supply their wants, when Heav'n can ſcarce ſupply !
Yet each reſuſal new detraction ſows,
And ev'ry hour procures increaſing foes.

Secure in conſcious rectitude to ſtand,
To ſteer the bark with unremitting hand,
When tempeſts riſe and blacken on the view,
To ſteer the bark is all that's left to do :
Though envy hiſs, and loud reſentment ſwell,
Be theirs to rage, and ours to govern well.

Yet think me not, Darget, reſolv'd to ſpare
One guilty monarch with fraternal care ;
Periſh, ye gods ! the proſtituted lays,
Which daub a tyrant with injurious praiſe.
The honeſt muſe ſhall ever learn to blame
The herd of vulgar kings, unknown to fame,
Pregnant with whim, or ſlumb'ring on a throne,
And to no kingdoms dreadful, but their own :
With ſuch the muſe declares eternal ſtrife,
Take then their portraits finiſh'd from the life.
A vulgar king —— But, lo ! thy looks betray
A moſt impatient wiſh to get away.
Thy wife prepares to chide thy late return,
Thy cook exclaims ; the roaſt begins to burn !
The very coachman thinks I keep you long,
I hear him cough, and ſmack his angry thong.

Well,

Well, go thy ways; but firſt, this maxim know,
That all eſtates find equal bliſs below.

The collection of poems, of which the above is a part,
was openly denied by its royal author, when it firſt made
its appearance in print. Whatever reaſon his Majeſty
may have for this denial, certain however it is, that
none acquainted in the leaſt with his writings, diſpute
the collection to be his.

A king who in this extraordinary manner undertakes
to inſtruct mankind, does honour not only to himſelf,
but to humanity. Though his motives for diſowning theſe
poems may be politic and wiſe, yet his motives for writing them are certainly laudable. Not led by the blind
admiration which influences the croud, we may ſafely
rank them among the few publications that do honour
to the preſent age; and had they been written by the
meaneſt ſubject, would have been applauded by all who
are poſſeſſed of any taſte, or who are pleaſed with ſtrong
and manly thinking.

But the genius of our royal author will appear in a
much ſtronger light, if we conſider, that ſeveral of the
above poems were wrote during the courſe of the preſent war; and that in the hurry and confuſion, the per-
plexities and cares, which neceſſarily muſt have attended
him through ſo many deſtructive and unſucceſsful cam-
paigns, his Majeſty ſhould ſtill find leiſure for an amuſe-
ment of ſo ſingular a nature. This ſhows a ſtrength of
genius almoſt without a parallel, a genius to which former ages can ſcarce produce an equal, and which the
preſent age muſt, with aſtoniſhment, admire.

HORACE,

HORACE, Ode 16. Book 2. imitated.

T HE weary failor calls for eafe,
   When winds turmoil the angry feas,
And not a moon or ftar to guide
His dreary courfe along the tide ;
When half the fky in fhowers defcends,
And wind the gilded ftreamer rends ;
Blefs'd he, within the hut, he cries,
Now bends in reft his peaceful eyes ;
Or hears the tempeft idly rave ;
No av'rice tempts him to the wave.

Turn to the noify camp your eye,
There care corrodes, and ftarts the figh.
Shew me the man among them all,
Who drove o'er Minden's plains the Gaul ;
When Broglio's ranks at diftance rife,
And cannon murmur through the fkies ;
But would forego the breath of fame,
And live at eafe without a name.

'Tis not the fafh, the gown, the robe,
Thefe gilded baits that catch the mob ;
Or tides of flatt'rers at the door,
Can paint with blifs the paffing hour ;
Or half the cares within controll,
And calm the tumults of the foul.

Nor

Nor can the dome or lofty wall,
Or guards that croud the tyrant's hall,
With all their inftruments of wars,
Exclude the dark, invading cares:
Around the bed of ftate they fly,
And dafh the guilty cup of joy.

More happy he! whofe guiltlefs mind,
Is to his native fields confin'd;
Blefs'd with his ftate; and craves no more
Than Heav'n allow'd his fires before;
Who fees his frugal table fpread,
Beneath the roof his fathers made;
No care, by day, difturbs his breaft,
He fleeps, by night, his brows in reft.

Whence all thefe fchemes, this wild uproar,
Since life itfelf fhall foon be o'er?
Why do we with advent'rous eyes,
See other funs in other fkies?
Or pant where Indian billows roll?
Or freeze beneath the arctic pole?
In vain we fly deftructive Care,
The monfter in our breafts we bear.

Go, then; forfake your calm retreat,
Cringe at the portals of the great;
Attend the gaudy venal train,
Throw virtue off, to raife your gain;

Or

Or fpread your canvas to the gale ;
Or court the mufes in the vale ;
If ftill in forrow you repine,
Fly for relief to whores and wine.

In vain you fly from inbred wo :
Care climbs the veffel's painted prow :
Care haunts the palace of the great,
And hovers round the dark retreat :
Care clouds the fair-one's lovely face,
And floats within the fparkling glafs.
Ev'n round the fprightly mufe it flies,
And taints the numbers as they rife.

If life you want undafh'd with wo,
Serene enjoy the inftant now ;
Nor ills you left behind deplore,
Nor eye the giant-grief before :
If Fortune fhines, enjoy the ray,
And fmile her very gloom away :
Let tempefts fweep and billows roar,
The ftorm of life fhall foon be o'er.

Some perifh in their youthful bloom ;
With age fome wither to the tomb ;
Heav'n, as a curfe, to fome fupplies
The years to others it denies ;
What can the longeft liver do,
But fee a greater train of wo ?

Be

Be yours in public life to fhine,
With all the glory of your line ;
To rule the battle's noify tide,
Or Britain's great concerns to guide;
Teach virtue to a venal throng,
While fenates liften to your tongue.
To me my fortune more fevere,
Has only giv'n a mind fincere ;
A fpark of genius to pafs o'er
The tedious dulnefs of the hour ;
A foul that can a knave defpife,
And eye the great with carelefs eyes.

++++++++++++++++++++ ++++++++++++++++++++++++++

HORACE, Ode 10. Book 2. imitated.

To a FRIEND.

WHen tempefts fweep and billows roll,
And winds contend along the pole ;
When o'er the deck afcends the fea,
And half the fheet is torn away ;
Shew me the man among the crew,
Who would not change his place with you ;
Prefer the quiet of the plain
To all the riches of the main.

Thrice

Thrice happy he! and he alone,
Who makes the golden mean his own;
Whose life is neither ebb or flow,
Nor rises high nor sinks too low:
He prides not in the envy'd wall,
Nor pines in Want's deserted hall;
His careless eyes with ease behold
The star, the string, and hoarded gold.

Unlike the venal sons of pow'r;
They rise, but rise to fall the more.
When faction rends the public air,
And Pitt shall tumble from his sphere,
In privacy secluded, you
Scarce feel which way the tempest blew.

Storms rend the lofty tow'r in twain,
And bow the poplar to the plain;
The hills are wrapt in clouds on high,
And feel th' artillery of the sky;
When not a breath the valley wakes,
Or curls the surface of the lakes.

When storms on Fortune's ocean lowr,
And rolling billows lash the shore;
When lov'd allies return to clay,
And paltry riches wing their way;
The faithless mob, the perjur'd whore,
That hover'd round thy pelf before,

L   Fall

Fall gradual down the ebbing tide ;
Thy dog, the laft, forfakes thy fide :
Retire within ; enjoy thy mind ;
There, what they all deny'd thee, find.
When Fortune threats to fly, be gay,
And puff the fickle thing away.
Nor ftill it lowrs ; the tempeft flies,
The golden fun defcends the fkies ;
The gale is living in the grafs,
In gentler furges roll the feas.
But wifely thou contract the fail,
And catch but half the breathing gale ;
Be cautious ftill of Fortune's wiles,
Avoid the Siren when fhe fmiles ;
With prudence laugh her gloom away,
And truft her leaft when fhe looks gay.

✢✢✢✢ ✢✢✢✢✢✢✢✢✢✢✢✢✢✢✢✢✢✢✢✢✢✢✢✢✢✢✢✢✢✢

The C H O I C E.

DID Fortune, what to few fhe'll give,
Allow me make my choice to live ;
I would not feek an envy'd feat,
Or daily vifits of the great ;
Nor yet would my ambition fall
To meagre Want's deferted hall ;
To each extreme alike a foe,
Too low for high, too high for low.

For

For ufe, not fhew, my houfe would ftand
Amid a fpot of fertile land;
A lake below; around a wood;
Here bend a rock —— there rufh a flood.
A mountain would in profpect rife,
And bear the grey mift to the fkies.
When in fome dark retreat I fit,
Be near a friend, a man of wit,
Of heart fincere and converfe free,
The lover of mankind and me,
Who, fhould the world tumultuous roar,
Could calmly fee the ftorm afhore,
Nor e'er admit a longing figh
To vex my privacy and I.

Here would I pafs my blamelefs days,
Belov'd of virtue and of eafe;
Here die in peace, and lie unknown
Without a monument or ftone.
My friend might fhed one pious tear;
My image in his bofom bear;
Might breathe, in verfe, his tender moan,
But breathe unto himfelf alone;
I envy to the world my name,
And puff away the ftrumpet Fame.

Written

Written on a BIRTH-DAY.

Alas the years! how fwift they roll,
How fwift they fly to Death's dark goal!
And let them roll, and let them fly,
I die but once —— and let me die.
Arriv'd at laft at twenty-two,
What honours rife upon my brow?
What have I done to raife my name,
And fend to future times my fame?
No matter what —— for this confoles,
That fame is but the breath of fools.
And what, alas! a name can do, .
When I am cold, when I am low?
Shall I come back to hear my lays
Excite the critic's after-praife?
Behold me quoted in Reviews,
Or pofted up to fame in news?
Let Fame deny or grant the bays,
No cenfure I fhall feel, nor praife.
Why fhould I then deftroy my peace,
Or purchafe fame with lofs of eafe?
But ftill the foft Aönian maid
Invites me, fmiling, to the fhade:
" One fong ere you lay by the lyre,
" Myfelf my poet will infpire."
Away! —— I own your pow'r no more,
Away! —— thou proftituted whore.

Your

Your charming fimpers, artful fmiles,
Perfuafive voice and little wiles,
No more fhall caufe me hunt for fame,
Or feek that empty fhade,——a name.

The MONUMENT.

IN vain we toil for lafting fame,
 Or give to other times our name;
The buft itfelf fhall foon be gone,
The figure moulder from the ftone;
The plaintive ftrain, the moving lay,
Like thofe they mourn, at laft decay:
My name, a furer way fhall live,
A furer way, my fair can give:
In her dear mem'ry let me live alone;
When NISA dies, I wifh not to be known.

VERSES

VERSES sent to a YOUNG LADY, with some TRANSLATIONS from the ERSE.

BEhold, fair maid, what Nature could inspire,
When Albion's lovely dames confess'd their fire;
When love was stranger to the guise of art,
And virgins spoke the language of the heart;
When sweet simplicity, with charms display'd,
Confirm'd the bands which beauty first had made.

On rocks they liv'd among the savage kind,
But little of the rock was in their mind;
They felt the call of nature in their heart,
And Pity wept when Beauty shot the dart:
Each maid, with sorrow, saw her conquests rise,
And drown'd with tears the lightning of her eyes.

When the lov'd youth appear'd with manly charms,
And call'd the blooming beauty to his arms;
To meet his gen'rous flame the maid wou'd fly,
Nor did the tongue, what eyes confess'd, deny.
" No toils could her from his dear side remove;
" She shar'd his dangers, as she shar'd his love.
" With him against the chace she bent the bow;
" In fields of death with him she met the foe;
" If pierc'd with wounds, a mournful sight he lay,
" With tears she wash'd the gory tide away;

" And

" And decent in the tomb her hero laid,
" And as fhe blefs'd him living, mourn'd him dead."

In thee, bleft nymph, indulgent Nature join'd
The face of beauty with the tender mind ;
In thee the prefent virtues we behold,
With all the charms of Albion's dames of old :
But be their forrow to themfelves alone,
As thine their beauty, be their woes their own.

Too oft, in times of old, did War's alarms,
Tear lovely Youth from Beauty's folding arms!
Too oft the early tears of fpoufes flow,
And blooming widows beat their breafts of fnow.
But when the happy youth of form divine,
At once the fav'rite of the world and thine,
Enjoys unrivall'd all that heav'n of charms,
Death late defcend! ——Avoid him hoftile arms !
Let growing pleafures crown each rifing year,
Still be that cheek unfullied with a tear ;
That heart no pang but of affection know ;
That ear be ftranger to the voice of wo.

When Time itfelf fhall bid that beauty fly,
And light'ning arm no more that lovely eye ;
May the bright legacy fucceffive fall,
And thy lov'd fons and daughters fhare it all ;
Thy fons be ev'ry virgin's fecret care,
Thy lovely daughters like the mother fair ;
The firft in prudence emulate their fire ;
The laft, like thee, fet all the world on fire.

The

The C A V E:

Written in the Highlands.

THE wind is up, the field is bare;
　　Some hermit lead me to his cell,
Where Contemplation, lonely fair,
　　With bleſs'd Content has choſe to dwell.

Behold! it opens to my ſight,
　　Dark in the rock; beſide the flood;
Dry fern around obſtructs the light;
　　The winds above it move the wood.

Reflected in the lake I ſee
　　The downward mountains and the ſkies,
The flying bird, the waving tree,
　　The goats that on the hills ariſe.

The grey-cloak'd herd drives on the cow;
　　The ſlow-pac'd fowler walks the heath;
A freckled pointer ſcours the brow;
　　A muſing ſhepherd ſtands beneath.

Curve o'er the ruin of an oak,
　　The wood-man lifts his ax on high,
The hills re-echo to the ſtroke;
　　I ſee, I ſee the chivers fly.

Some

Some rural maid, with apron full,
  Brings fuel to the homely flame ;
I fee the fmoky columns roll,
  And through the chinky hut the beam.

Befide a ftone o'ergrown with mofs,
  Two well-met hunters talk at eafe ;
Three panting dogs befide repofe ;
  One bleeding deer is ftretch'd on grafs.

A lake, at diftance, fpreads to fight,
  Skirted with fhady forefts round,
In midft an ifland's rocky height,
  Suftains a ruin once renown'd.

One tree bends o'er the naked walls,
  Two broad-wing'd eagles hover nigh,
By intervals a fragment falls,
  As blows the blaft along the fky.

Two rough-fpun hinds the pinnace guide,
  With lab'ring oars along the flood ;
An angler bending o'er the tide,
  Hangs from the boat th' infidious wood.

Befide the flood, beneath the rocks,
  On grafly bank two lovers lean ;
Bend on each other am'rous looks,
  And feem to laugh and kifs between.

The

The wind is ruftling in the oak;
 They feem to hear the tread of feet;
They ftart, they rife, look round the rock;
 Again they fmile, again they meet.

But fee! the grey mift from the lake
 Afcends upon the fhady hills;
Dark ftorms the murm'ring forefts fhake,
 Rain beats —— refound a hundred rills.

To Damon's homely hut I fly;
 I fee it fmoking o'er the plain:
When ftorms are paft —— and fair the fky,
 I'll often feek my cave again.

✛✛✛✛✛✛✛✛✛✛✛✛✛✛✛✛✛✛✛✛✛✛✛✛✛✛✛✛✛✛✛✛✛✛✛

-

FRAGMENTS from TYRTÆUS.

FRAGMENT I.

I Call the man unworthy of my praife,
 Who wins the palm in wreftling or the race;
Shou'd he excel in bulk and ftrength mankind,
Or in the courfe outftrip the Thracian wind;
Though Nature gave him Tithon's form divine,
And Afia pour'd him wealth from ev'ry mine;

Though

Though Pelops' wide domains to him belong,
And more, Adraftus' eloquence of tongue;
Though Fortune ev'ry other virtue gave,
And yet deny the greateft —— to be brave.
And brave alone is he, who can fuftain
The wild confufion of the bloody plain;
Can death and wounds behold with dire delight,
And fhady legions moving to the fight.
For he alone a lafting name can raife,
And crown his early years with martial praife,
Who in the front of battle ftands unmov'd,
The bulwark of the country which he lov'd;
And loving, prodigal of life, to die,
Avoids no evil more than bafely fly.
His great example fhall the hoft infpire,
And thoufands follow actions they admire.

He turns the phalanx of the foe to flight,
And rules with martial art, the tide of fight: .
And when he falls amid the field of fame,
He leaves behind a great and lafting name;
His fire, his country fhall with joy furround
His corfe, and read their glory in his wound.
Both young and old fhall fing his dirge of wo;
And his long fun'ral all the town purfue:
His tomb fhall be rever'd: his children fhine
Through ev'ry age, a long-extended line.
Ne'er fhall his glory fade, or ceafe his fame;
Though laid in duft, immortal is his name,

Who

Who never from the field of battle flies,
But for his children and his country dies.
But if the fable hand of Death he fhun,
Returning victor, with his glory won;
By young and old rever'd, his life he'll lead,
And full of honour fink among the dead:
Or with his growing years his fame will grow,
And all fhall reverence his head of fnow.
The higher place from ev'ry youth he bears,
And age fhall quit him all the claim of years.
Who then defires to rife to fuch a hight,
Defires in vain, if he forget the fight.

FRAGMENT II.

YE, then, who boaft Alcides' race divine,
Be ftrong; great Jove fhall ne'er forfake his line.
Aided by Heav'n no human prowefs fear;
Exalt the fhady buckler to the war.
But, bent on fate, what danger need you fly,
Or fhun a death fo grateful to the fky?
Ye knew the horrid work of arms before,
The difmal fhock of battle oft ye bore;
Or when you fled, or when the field·you won,
In each reverfe to you is Fortune known.

For

For thofe who, in the front of battle, dare
Fight hand to hand, and bear the brunt of war,
But rarely fall. —— Though daftards fkulk behind,
The fate they fhun ftill haunts the cow'rdly kind.
What mind can well conceive, or tongue relate,
The ills unnam'd that on the truant wait?
To fhun his fate when from the field he flies,
Pierc'd from behind, th' inglorious coward dies.
When prone he lies and gafping on the ground,
What fhame, to fee behind the gaping wound!

But, firm to earth, let ev'ry warrior grow,
Strain his large limbs, and, lowring eye the foe;
Let ev'ry fhield, a mighty round, difplay'd
From head to foot the gather'd warrior fhade;
Each vig'rous hand the fpear protended hold,
When dreadful nodes above the cafque of gold.
To mighty deeds let each his arm extend,
Nor dread the darts his buckler may defend.
To diftance let him not project the fpear,
But manage hand to hand the work of war;
Shield clos'd to fhield, advance th' imbattled line,
Creft reach to creft, and cafque to helmet join;
When, breaft to breaft, are ftretch'd the ranks of war,
Hew them with fwords or break them with the fpear.
Ye, whom no heavy panoplies inclofe,
Difcharge, at diftance, ftones againft the foes,
And hurl with martial force the miffive fpear;
But near the phalanx, fhun the clofer war.

M   FRAG-

HOW graceful lies the brave man on the plain,
Cover'd with wounds, and for his country flain!
But ah! expell'd from home, how mean! how low!
Through foreign realms to lead a life of wo!
Strolling with parents funk in wieldlefs years,
A helplefs wife, and infants drown'd in tears!
Condemn'd to want and fhame, him all fhall hate,
And drive the wand'rer from the cloſing gate.
His form he fhall difgrace, his race, his blood,
By ills unnam'd and infamy purfu'd.
Nor only is the daftard loft to fame,
But, what is worfe, to all the fenfe of fhame.

But let us fight for Sparta while we may,
Nor fpare a life which foon muft pafs away.
Collect your bands, ye warriors, clofely fight;
Forget your fear; forget inglorious flight.
Let glory every martial bofom fill,
Nor value life when foes remain to kill.
Leave not the hoary vet'rans numb'd with age,
Where burns the combat, and the thickeſt rage:
What fhame! an aged warrior prone fhould lie,
Transfix'd with wounds, when younger men are by;
His beard transform'd, his wrinkled temples gray,
And breathe, in duft, his dauntlefs foul away?

Who

Who can his hands behold, with fhamelefs eyes,
Cov'ring his naked carcafs as he lies,
Decent in death ?—— But all things youth become,
Whom Nature covers with her faireft bloom ;
Graceful, in life, to men and womens eyes;
Graceful, in death, when on the field he lies.
Then, once engag'd, let ev'ry warrior grow
Firm to the earth, and lowr upon the foe.

++

ANACREON, Ode 4. tranflated.

ON beds of tender myrtles laid,
   Or melelot, fupinely fpread,
I'll quaff the bowl; and, neatly dreft,
Young Cupid fhall direct the feaft.
Come ! fill the bumper to the brim,
And heave away this load of time.
This little wheel of vital day
Shall fhortly roll itfelf away ;
And when we to the duft return,
How fmall our portion in the urn !
Why fhould you then anoint my ftone ?
Or earth with rich libations drown ?
No : rather let my fleeky hair
The fragrant oil and chaplet wear

M 2   While

While yet I live; with all her charms
Call too my fair-one to my arms;
And Love, before from hence I go,
To mingle with the shades below;
Here let me diffipate my care,
And leave my grief in upper air.

ANACREON, Ode 8.

BY night, on purple carpets spread,
When Bacchus hover'd in my head;
In dreams I seem'd to stretch the race
With virgins of the faireft face;
While taunting youths at diftance ftood,
As fair as of immortal blood;
And ridicul'd me for the fair,
But feem'd to wifh themfelves were there.
Unheeding I purfue my blifs,
And try to fnatch one bahny kifs,
When, all at once, the vifion fled,
And left me haplefs on the bed:
The promis'd blifs hung in my brain;
I turn'd, and wifh'd to fleep again.

In

In anfwer to a letter from DELIA.

TWice has the winter vex'd the main,
And twice the fummer parch'd the plain,
Since, abfent from his Delia's eyes,
Remote the haplefs poet fighs,
And fees the joylefs feafons roll,
Far from the charmer of his foul.

In vain, to fhroud thee from my eyes,
Or billows roll or mountains rife,
When, diving in the fecret fhade,
I fee, in thought, my charming maid
In all the light of beauty move,
As when fhe warm'd my heart to love :
Again her charms my foul furprife,
I feel the lightning of her eyes ;
Her marble neck, her hair behold
Like winding tides of melted gold ;
Still on her cheek the rofes glow,
Still fwells her breaft of heaving fnow.
The vifion flies, delufive all !
From what a height poor mortals fall !
I wake to care —— My fair no more
I fee ; —— The winds around me roar ;
Cold fhow'rs from fullen fkies defcend,
And ftorms the lofty foreft rend ;

I

I fly the tempeſt —— leave the plain,
But oh! from love I fly in vain.

In crouds wou'd I diſſolve my care,
The peace I ſeek, I find not there.
My abſent fair-one prompts my ſighs,
And calls the tears from both my eyes;
My heart beats thick againſt my ſide,
More ſwiftly rolls the crimſon tide;
I ſweat, I pant, my ears reſound,
And viſion dimly ſwims around.
I pine, I languiſh in my pain,
And ſcarce does half the man remain.

I eye the maids, the ſoft and gay,
And wiſh to look my ſoul away;
With other objects to ſupply
The fair, the adverſe fates deny;
Ill were my fair by them ſupply'd, ——
Their form diſguſts, but more their pride.
With haughty ſneer they ſeem to ſay,
Away, dull impudence! away!
You look, you ſigh and weep in vain;
Go; woo ſome trull upon the plain.
With conſcious ſhame I bluſh, I glow;
My Delia wou'd not uſe me ſo ——

A packet! —— 'tis my Delia's hand——
What would my lovely maid command?
Am I my fair-one's tender care?
Love me! —— What would you love, my dear?

No fair domains of mine are fpread,
No lofty villa rears its head;
No lowing herds are heard afar,
Nor neighs the courfer at my car;
No pageantry of ftate is mine,
I boaft no nobles in my line;
My numbers are admir'd by none,
Or by my partial maid alone;
No beauties on my limbs arife,
Nor arm'd with lightning are my eyes:
Love me! what would you love, my dear?
A gen'rous heart —— a mind fincere;
A foul that Fortune's frowns defies,
Nor flatters fools I muft defpife,
Is all I boaft, my charming fair!
Love me! —— what wou'd you love, my dear?

✛✛✛✛✛✛✛✛✛✛✛✛✛✛✛✛✛✛✛✛✛✛✛✛✛✛✛✛✛✛✛✛✛✛✛✛✛

A N I G H T - P I E C E.

'TIS night: and ftorms the foreft fhake;
Dark roll the billows on the lake;
The whirlwind fweeps; defcends the rain,
The torrents echo to the plain:
Through defert paths forlorn I ftray,
And not a moon to light my way;

No friendly ſtar with golden eye
Looks from the cieling of the ſky.

   Here ſounds an oak ; —— there ſpreads a plane ;
Above, the rock defends the rain ;
The murm'ring rill o'er pebbles flies,
The wind along the bramble ſighs :
A fox is howling on the rock,
A ſcreech-owl on a blaſted oak :
The paſſing meteor lights the vale ;
A ſpirit whiſpers on the gale,
Or beck'ning longs to breathe its care ;
And ghaſtly horror rides the air.

   A ruin ! 'Twas of old the ſeat
Of heroes now reſign'd to fate ;
Where often mirth relax'd the ſoul,
And midnight crown'd the roſy bowl ;
Where ſprightly muſic ſwell'd the ſound,
While blooming beauty tript around.
They vaniſh'd, as they ne'er had been,
No lyre is heard, no maid is ſeen,
No more the tuneful lyriſt warms,
Death long ſince rifled Beauty's charms ;
No warrior's martial ſize is ſhown,
Time moulders down the very ſtone ;
With ev'ry blaſt the fragments fill,
And winds are bluſt'ring in the hall.

                   Unhappy

Unhappy man! how fhort his date,
He fprings to light, and finks in fate;
Ev'n from the womb, the tomb is feen;
And forrow fills the fpace between.
Bid paltry riches glut his eye,
Or empty glory raife him high;
Bid him in wrangling fenates glow,'
Or turn the batt'ry on the foe;
Yet, high or low, 'tis mankind's lot,
To live in grief, and die forgot.

Go, on the ftone infcribe thy name,
And to the marble truft thy fame;
Bid half the mountain form thy tomb,
The wonder of the times to come;
The mound fhall fink, the ftone decay,
The fculptur'd figure wear away;
The buft that proudly fpeaks thy praife,
Some fhepherd's future cote may raife;
While, fmiling round, his infant fon
Admires the figures on the ftone.

A tomb its dreary honour fhows!
Three ftones exalt their heads of mofs;
A buft, half-funk in earth, appears,
The rude remains of former years;
Dry tufts of grafs around it rife,
The wind along the brufhwood fighs,
Now peeping from the cloudy pole,
The moon has filver'd o'er the whole.

Here,

Here, hoar Tradition tells, repofe
Two youths the dread of Albion's foes,
Of other times the grace and pride,
Who fav'd their country when they dy'd;
But rolling Time has loft their name,
So faithlefs is the breath of Fame.
That light! it iffues from the cot,
Be grief fufpended,— care forgot:
There Nifa for her lover fighs,
And rolls on night her wifhful eyes:
Why has my ling'ring rover ftay'd?
I come, I come, my lovely maid,
To feaft my eyes on all your charms,
And lofe my forrow in your arms.

❖❖❖❖❖❖❖❖❖❖❖❖❖❖❖❖❖❖❖❖❖❖❖❖❖❖❖❖❖❖❖❖

A Letter to a Young Lady.

WHen half the nation round Almira fighs,
    And fenfe fecures the conquefts of her eyes,
Why bids the nymph a mufe unknown to fame
To grace her numbers with fo fair a name?
Or would the maid add luftre to my lays?
Or fhew the world how weakly I can praife?

The mufe difclaim'd, and all the pow'rs of fong,
The rapture vanifh'd, and the lyre unftrung;

I

I left to other bards their groves of bays,
And facrific'd my hopes of fame to eafe.
Nor Delia's charms cou'd bid my numbers rife,
Nor caught my foul the fire of Chloe's eyes;
On Mira's cheek in vain did rofes glow,
And Chloris hear'd, unfung, her breaft of fnow;
Almira only could my breaft inflame,
Were but my ftrength proportion'd to my theme.

Grant then I fung, what honour could I pay,
Where ev'ry grace difplay'd prevents the lay?
Thee firft in beauty, fighing thoufands own;
And thou art ftranger to thy worth alone:
Charms after charms in fair fucceffion rife,
Thy wit purfues the progrefs of thine eyes;
Each love-fick youth, without the poet's art,
Beholds enough to rob him of his heart;
The mufe defpairs to make thee brighter fhine,
Or give one beauty not already thine.

Permit me then, fince ufelefs are my lays,
To give my adoration for my praife;
With other youths, the pleafing pain to prove;
Tho' hope, alas, can never lodge with love:
Let me admire the charms I'll ne'er poffefs;
And eye, in rapture, what I can't exprefs.

ADELLA:

ADELLA: A Poem.

BE forrow banifh'd, give not all your bloom,
Thus to be prey'd on by the canker Grief:
Go, take a manly firmnefs to your breaft;
Ah! ftray not penfive by the lonely ftream,
And feek not by the folitary moon,
The gloomy umbrage of the foreft dark;
Too foft'ning for a heart furcharg'd with wo.
Tell me, when all is awful filence round,
Does not the deep impreffion of your anguifh
Bear with redoubled force upon your mind?
Truft not fuch fcenes, but ftill at redd'ning dawn,
Sweep with your hounds acrofs the ftream-fed vale,
Burft o'er the hills, and plunge into the plain;
Then when the greenwood rings with joyous fhout,
While jolly echoes fwell the clam'rous din,
Let mirth and gladnefs twine around your foul:
If this delight not, let your barbed fhaft,   -
Swift cut the air, and ftop the flying deer;
Or ride upon the bofom of the wave,
Dart the ftrong arm, and fhoot acrofs the furge:
Hence fhall your mind, and nerves new ftrength acquire;
For exercife improves the mental pow'rs,
And lifts each languid burthen from the heart.
Come, let the joys of fweet fociety,
And mirthful converfe, win you to yourfelf;
For folitude does ftill engender wo,

Deep-

Deep-mufing Sadnefs waits upon her fteps,
Black Melancholy breathes her poifon round,
And darkens all the chearful face of day.
Your caufe of grief is great; but yet, compar'd
With mine, feems lighter than the weakeft breeze
That gently fwells along the fummer-lake,
Or fcarcely ftirs the tall tree's topmoft bough.
Much, much indeed, I've fuffer'd; yet the hand
Of lenient Time, the fureft friend of Grief,
Has melted down my keener fenfe of wo
Into a not unpleafing fort of fadnefs.
Perhaps when you have heard my forrowing tale,
You'll hold your pains in leffer eftimation.
If, whilft I fpeak, my falt'ring tongue fhould ftop,
Or the big tear fhould roll adown my cheek,
Impute my weaknefs to a feeling heart,
Too feeling ftill, though much inur'd to wo :
For Time, my friend, although it foftens much,
Yet cannot fteal us from our fuff'rings quite ;
But leaves a kind of luxury of fadnefs,
On which th' unhappy feed.   Adarmon, hear.

   My fame, my fortune, and my anceftry,
You know, and to recount them would be vain;
Suffice it for to fay, there's none more great.
Of hill, and dale, of rock-encircled plain,
Of rolling rivers, and of black'ning woods,
And bleating flocks, I amply am poffefs'd:
The orient fun, what time with keeneft ray
He burfts indignant thro' the flying mifts,

Difclofing

Difclofing firſt the high o'er-hanging cliffs,
Next ſparkling in the many-tinctur'd dew-drop,
Sees not a nobler manſion grace the land,
Than mine, which riſes on yon green-ſlop'd hill.
Twice twenty ſummer ſuns are now elaps'd,
Since once, 'twas in the ſpring, a dreadful ſtorm
Defac'd the beauties of the riſing year;
Three days with force it rag'd, but on the fourth
Was huſh'd; with haſte I left my early bed,
The beach I ſought, and mark'd the ſwelling waves
In long ſucceſſion rolling to the ſhore.   .
As ſoft I ſtole along the cavern'd banks,
My eyes wide wand'ring o'er the blue-ting'd main,
Methought I ſpy'd, upon the beating ſurge,
A human figure; in at once I ruſh'd,
Claſp'd in my arms I brought it to the land.
But gueſs, Adarmon, gueſs my ſtrong amaze,
When I ſurvey'd the burthen which I bore;
A woman! pallid, faint, and almoſt dead,
But yet ſo fair in that cold marble ſtate,
With graces ſo peculiarly her own,
That from that hapleſs hour I date my love.
With tend'reſt care I brought her to herſelf:
Her eyes ſhe open'd, blue as was the deep
From which I had the happineſs to ſave her.
With trembling ſteps I led her to my caſtle:
Much by the way ſhe ſpoke, and wav'd her hand;
The ſpeech was all unknown; but then ſo ſoft,
So ſweet, ſo full of ſoul-enchanting ſound,
That all my liſt'ning faculties were charm'd.

Why

Why need I tell the progrefs of our loves?
I quickly learnt her pure melodious fpeech,
And woo'd her in her own harmonious words.
Oh, 'twas a time of great and true delight!
I ftrove to frame my voice to gentlenefs,
To teach my fteps a grace unknown before,
And pleafe, in ev'ry thing, the fair Adella.
As once we walk'd, I eager fought to know
From whence fhe came, and how the fport of winds
Drove on my fhore, I was fo blefs'd as fave her.
Behold, fhe faid, where far acrofs the main,
Mix'd with the horizon, my country feems,
Like low-hung clouds light hov'ring o'er the deep,
There harmlefsly my infancy was pafs'd;
Thefe happy years too rapid fly away;
At laft, grown up, I hourly was befieg'd,
By many a various lover, for my hand.
Unhappily my father pitch'd on Merdin;
Rich, it is true, but quite a blot of nature,
Mifhapen, envious, and full of years;
Unknown to him the elegance of love,
The pure ingenuous fympathy of foul
That binds in willing chains accordant minds.
Opprefs'd with fear, I brib'd a fhip to waft me
To a fair ifland where my brother dwelt,
Who ftill has lov'd me from my early years.
Soon as I left my rugged father's coaft,
The howling tempeft rofe; the reft you know.
All yet, my friend, was happinefs and joy;
Day after day I ftole into her heart;

She

She would not truft me in the lonely gloom,
Where nods the foreft, and where pours the ftream;
Whene'er I fpoke, a crimfon flufh'd her cheek,
A gentle trembling fhook her tender frame ;
Her voice, her ev'ry action told her love ;
I mark'd the figns, and found my foul was blefs'd.
Now, now, Adarmon, comes the voice of wo :
Why hangs the fweat upon my clay-cold brow ?
Why rufhes all her beauty on my mind ?
Why fail my eyes? why wildly beats my heart ?
Alas ! this recollection quite unmans me :
Yet let me make an effort for to end.
One fated morn I left the fair Adella,
And all in fpirits tempted far the chace,
Nor till the ev'ning crimfon'd in the weft,
Did I return ; then judge my deep diftrefs,
When firft I learnt that I had loft Adella,
By lawlefs brutal ruffians torn away.
I arm'd my vaffals, and purfu'd the foe.
Loud blew the ftormy wind upon our coaft :
Stop'd by the gale I quickly overtook them.
When Merdin faw his hopes of flight were vain,
High on the deck the cruel monfter ftood,
The fair Adella trembling in his hand,
Thou ne'er fhalt make him happy, loud he cry'd,
And inftant plung'd his fabre in her breaft.
Inflam'd with rage, I flew him on the fpot :
Poor, poor revenge ; he fhould have tafted death
In ev'ry cruel form of vary'd pain.
I rais'd the bleeding fair-one in my arms :

Her

Her languid eyes beheld me e'er they clos'd ;
I heard the laſt faint murmurs of her voice ;
She feebly claſp'd my hand, and ſmiling dy'd.
Oh! many a ling'ring hour ſince that I've wept ;
The ſlow returning years ſtill found me wretched :
How could I ever bear her fatal loſs!
The ſtars that tremble through a ſunmer-ſhow'r,
Ne'er match'd the heav'nly radiance of her eyes ;
More ſnowy boſom never heav'd a ſigh,
More melting voice ne'er roll'd enchanting ſound ;
She pour'd inſtruction from her vermil lip ;
Grace, eaſe, and majeſty adorn'd her ſtep :
And yet the mournful parting I ſurviv'd.
O'er ev'ry hill the voice of ſorrow flew ;
The gloomy ſhore on which the wild wave beats
Has heard my loud complainings ; now they're huſh'd ;
Sooth'd by the hand of Time my ſuff'rings ceaſe,
My ſoul-embitter'd hours are now no more,
Ceas'd the ſwift tear, and huſh'd the deep-breath'd ſigh.
Know then, Adarmon, that your woes will end,
Your folded arms, your pallid looks will fly,
And pleaſing melancholy will remain.

MORNA:

MORNA: A Poem.

MY burſting heart is torn with racking pain,
Black horrors madden in my raging brain.
Narmon, you aſk the ſtory of my woes,
What rends my boſom, whence my anguiſh flows,
Why glooms oppreſſive darken in my eyes,
Roll the ſlow hours, and blaſt them as they riſe?
Oh, I am ſteep'd in guilt, am bath'd in blood,
Deſpair pours o'er me in a black'ning flood!
Morna I lov'd, Morna the beauteous maid,
With equal fondneſs all my love repaid.
Her voice was ſofter than the morning-gale,
That ſweeps with tardy ſtep the deep'ning vale;
Her breath was ſweeter than the breath of flow'rs,
When all their ſcents are waken'd by the ſhow'rs;
The blue that trembles thro' the whit'ning ſky,
Such melting blue roll'd liquid in her eye;
Her ſmile was genial as the wiſh'd-for ſpring,
When blow the bloſſoms, and the gay birds ſing:
And yet I kill'd her! hide me, mountains, hide,
Or plunge me in a never-ebbing tide!
Oh, bear me in a tempeſt of the wind,
And waft me from this madneſs of the mind!
Morna for me had long her love confeſs'd,
And, often urg'd, had vow'd ſhe'd make me bleſs'd;

When

When lo, to blaſt our joys, young Rodnor came;
He ſaw, he lov'd, and quick avow'd his flame.
The graceful Rodnor, arm'd with ev'ry art,
To ſoften virtue, and ſeduce the heart;.
His manly ſtep was firm, erect,. and bold,
His ſhoulders were o'erſpread with.locks of gold :-
Yet was his breaſt a ſtore of endleſs wiles,
At pleaſure he could dreſs his face in ſmiles.
Diſtruſt I then receiv'd within my breaſt ;
The days ſeem'd long, my nights were robb'd of reſt ;
Suſpicious and revengeful I became,
I thought that Morna eager met his flame;
I thought I ſaw a mutual paſſion riſe,
Glow on her cheeks, and ſparkle in her eyes.
Suſpicion, deepeſt torment of the brain,
The ſtrength of miſery, the ſoul of pain,
Rack'd my torn hours, pour'd venom on my mind,
Deaf to all love, to all compaſſion blind.
I ſought young Rodnor panting for the fight :
He fled, with Morna, partner of his flight ;
Swift as the lightning from the burſting cloud,
When rolling thunders echo long and loud,
I came upon them on the verdant plain ;
The traitor Rodnor inſtantly was ſlain ;.
Fire in my face, and fury in my eyes,
I heeded not the lovely Morna's cries ;.
Low at my feet for mercy ſhe implor'd,
Thro' her fair breaſt I paſs'd the ſhining ſword.
I die, ſhe feebly cry'd ; but, ere I go,
Learn your miſtake, and tremble when you know,

'Twas

'Twas with reluctance Rodnor I obey'd,
By force conftrain'd, and for my life afraid.
She ceas'd; a palenefs all her charms o'ercaft,
Faint, and more faint fhe grew, then breath'd her laft.
From that curfs'd hour I'm torn with paffions wild,
Fierce feas feem calm, and winter-whirlwinds mild.
Roll on, ye hours, and never end, oh Time,
I'll curfe myfelf with life to feel my crime!
Bright Sun, behold a wretch in torture rife;
Black Night, ne'er fhut in fleep that wretch's eyes.
When rifing winds the wafte of waves deform,
When founding forefts bend beneath the ftorm,
When all his tempefts howling Winter blows,
Beftrides the north, and drives along in fnows;
Fir'd with defpair, I'll feek the favage fcene,
Where murder ting'd with blood the verdant green;
My Morna's vifionary ghoft fhall rife,
Frefh from her wound, and glide before my eyes;.
To blaft me wholly, curfe me with a fmile,
And added tortures in my bofom pile.
My burfting heart is torn with racking pain,
Black horrors madden in my raging brain.

The fourth Pastoral of VIRGIL,

Attempted in ENGLISH VERSE.

By the Rev. Mr J. B ——.

P O L L I O.

Sicilian mufe, fublimer ftrains infpire,
And warm my bofom with a nobler fire!
All take not pleafure in the rural fcene,
In lowly tamarifks and forefts green.
If fylvan themes we fing, then let our lays
Deferve a conful's ear, a conful's praife.

The age comes on, that future age of gold,
In Cuma's myftic prophecies foretold.
The years begin their mighty courfe again,
The virgin now returns, and Saturn's happy reign.
Now one of heav'nly offspring from on high,
Defcends to earth, and quits his native fky.—
Thy Phœbus reigns; Lucina, lend thy aid;
Nor be his birth, his glorious birth delay'd !
An iron race fhall then no longer rage,
But all the world regain the golden age.
This child, (the joy of nations !) fhall be born,
Thy confulfhip, O Pollio, to adorn;
Thy confulfhip thefe happy times fhall prove,
And fee thefe mighty months begin to move.

Guilt,

Guilt, and its dire remains, by thee ſhall ceaſe,
No fears henceforth alarm the world's eternal peace.

The ſon with heroes and with gods ſhall ſhine,
And lead, inroll'd with them, the life divine.
He o'er the peaceful nations ſhall preſide,
And his ſire's virtues ſhall his ſceptre guide.
For thee, the earth her ſweeteſt herbs ſhall yield,
And flow'rs ſpontaneous deck the fragrant field ;
Here wand'ring ivy ſhall its leaves diſplay,
Acanthus there, in ſmiling beauty gay.
Homeward the goats with loaded dugs ſhall come,
The fearleſs herds with harmleſs lions roam :
Sweet flow'rs ſhall ſpring thy cradle to embrace,
The ſerpent die, with all his pois'nous race ;
Each noxious herb for ever ceaſe to grow,
Aſſyrian balm on ev'ry buſh ſhall blow.

But when thy father's deeds thy youth ſhall fire,
And to great actions all thy ſoul inſpire ;
When thou ſhalt read of heroes and of kings,
And mark the glory that from virtue ſprings ;
Then ſhall the fields wave wide with golden grain,
Unbidden crops with plenty crown the plain ;
With purple grapes the loaded thorn ſhall bend,
And ſhow'rs of honey from the oak deſcend.
Nor yet, old Fraud ſhall wholly be effac'd ;
Navies, for wealth, ſhall tempt the watry waſte ;
Proud cities fenc'd with lofty walls appear,
And cruel ſhares the furrow'd glebe ſhall tear :

Another

Another Tiphys, o'er the fwelling tide,
With fteady fkill the bounding fhip fhall guide;
Another Argo, with the flow'r of Greece,
From Colchos' fhore fhall waft the golden fleece;
Again the world fhall hear war's loud alarms,
And great Achilles fhine again in arms.

When riper years thy ftrengthen'd nerves fhall brace,
And o'er thy limbs diffufe a manly grace;
No more the mariner fhall plow the deep,
Nor load with foreign wares the trading fhip;
Each country fhall abound with ev'ry ftore,
Nor need the products of another fhore.
Henceforth no plough the fertile foil fhall bear,
No pruning-hook the tender vine fhall tear;
The hufbandman, with toil no longer broke,
Shall loofe his ox for ever from the yoke.
No more the wool a foreign dye fhall feign,
But purple flocks fhall graze the flow'ry plain;
In native gold array'd, the ram fhall tread,
And fcarlet lambs fhall wanton on the mead.
In concord join'd with fate's unalter'd law,
The deftinies thefe happy times forefaw;
They bade the facred fpindle fwiftly run,
And haften the aufpicious ages on.

Oh, dear to all thy kindred gods above!
O thou, the offspring of immortal Jove!
Receive thy dignities, begin thy reign,
And o'er the world extend thy wide domain.

See

See nature's frame exulting with delight!
Ocean, and earth, and heav'n's unbounded height!
See nations yet unborn with joy behold
Thy glad approach, and hail the age of gold!

Oh! would th' immortals lend a length of days,
And give a foul fublime to fing thy praife!
Would Heav'n this breaft, this raptur'd breaft, inflame
With ardor equal to the mighty theme!
Not Orpheus with diviner tranfports glow'd,
When all her fire his mother-mufe beftow'd;
Nor loftier numbers flow'd from Linus' tongue,
Although his fire Apollo gave the fong.
Though Pan, in prefence of Arcadian fwains,
Should try his utmoft fkill, his nobleft ftrains;
Arcadian judges would prefer my mufe,
Nor would the god my victory refufe.

Repay a parent's cares, O lovely boy,
And greet thy mother with a fmile of joy:
Of ten long months the tedious round fhe pafs'd,
While irkfome qualms her penfive foul opprefs'd.
If cruel fate the parent's blifs denies,
If no fond joy fits fmiling in thy eyes;
No nymph of heav'nly birth fhall crown thy love,
Nor fhalt thou fhare th' immortal feafts above.

The

The Fifth Paſtoral of VIRGIL,
Attempted in ENGLISH VERSE.

By the ſame.

MENALCAS, MOPSUS.

MENALCAS.

Since you with ſkill can touch the tender reed;
Since few my voice or verſes can exceed;
In this refreſhing ſhade ſhall we recline,
Where hazles with the lofty elms combine.

MOPSUS.

Your riper age a due reſpect requires;
'Tis mine to yield to what my friend deſires;
Whether you chooſe the zephyr's cooling breeze,
That ſhakes the floating ſhadows of the trees;
Or the deep-ſhaded grot's tranquil retreat,
And ſee yon cave ſcreen'd from the ſcorching heat,
Where the wild vine its curling tendrils waves,
Whoſe grapes glow ruddy thro' the quiv'ring leaves.

MENALCAS.

Of all the ſwains that to our hills belong,
Amyntas only vies with you in ſong.

M o p s u s.

What tho' with me that haughty fwain fhould vie,
Who proudly dares Appollo's felf defy?

M e n a l c a s.

Begin: let Alcon's praife infpire your ftrains,
Or Codrus' death, or Phyllis' am'rous pains:
Begin, whatever theme your mufe prefer;
To feed the kids, be, Tityrus, thy care.

M o p s u s.

I rather will rehearfe that fong of wo,
Which on the beech I carv'd not long ago:
(I carv'd and trill'd by turns the mournful lay).
And let Amyntas match me, if he may.

M e n a l c a s.

As flender willows where the olive grows,
Or leaflefs fhrubs when near the fcarlet rofe;
Such, if the judgment I have form'd be true,
Such is Amyntas when compar'd with you.

M o p s u s.

No more, Menalcas! we delay too long;
The grot's dim fhade invites my promis'd fong.

" When Daphnis lay extended on the plain,
" By cruel deftiny untimely flain;
" The nymphs bemoan'd his death with weeping eyes,
" The woods, the rivers, heard their ceafelefs fighs.

" His

" His mother came, and all diftracted prefs'd
" The clay-cold carcafe to her throbbing breaft ;
" Frantic with grief fhe wail'd his haplefs fate,
" Rav'd at the ftars, and heav'n's relentlefs hate.
" 'Twas then the fwains in deep defpair forfook
" Their pining flocks, nor led them to the brook ;
" The pining flocks for him their paftures flight,
" Nor herbag'd plains, nor cooling ftreams invite.
" The doleful news foon reach'd the Libyan fhores,
" And lions mourn'd in deep repeated roars.
" The woods and groves his cruel lot bewail,
" And plaintive hills repeat the melancholy tale.
" 'Twas he who firft th' Armenian tygers broke,
" Tam'd their fell rage, and join'd them to the yoke.
" He firft with ivy wrapt the Thyrfus round,
" And made the hills with Bacchus' rites refound.
" As vines adorn the trees which they entwine,
" As purple grapes give beauty to the vine,
" As fertile fields are grac'd with yellow corns,
" And as the lordly bull the herd adorns ;
" Thy godlike virtues thus diffufe a grace,
" And fhed diftinguifh'd luftre on thy race.
" When cruel fate bereft us of the fwain,
" Phœbus and Pales left the mournful plain.
" Now weeds and wretched tares the crop fubdue,
" Where ftore of richeft wheat but lately grew.
" Narciffus' purple flow'r no more is feen,
" No more the gentle vi'let decks the green ;
" Thiftles, for thefe, the blafted meadow yields,
" And thorns and briars over-run the fields.

" Ye

" Ye fhepherds, ftrew with leaves the holy ground,
" With folemn fhades the filver fprings furround.
" Thefe rites to Daphnis' memory we owe;
" 'Twas Daphnis' laft command when here below.
" Erect a tomb in honour of his name,
" With this infcription to record his fame.
" *With Daphnis' name the fwains this tomb adorn,*
" *Whofe high renown above the fkies is born :*
" *His fock was fair, he faireft on the plain,*
" *The pride, the glory of the fylvan reign.*"

MENALCAS.

O heav'nly bard, fo melting are thy lays,
Thy fong fuch pleafure to my foul conveys,
As balmy flumbers in the verdant fhade,
When wearinefs and heat the limbs invade :
Sweeter to me thy fadly-pleafing ftrain,
Than running riv'lets to the thirfty fwain.
To raife the vocal lay, to touch the reed,
Your mafter only could your fkill exceed :
Blefs'd youth ! your merit fhall obtain a name,
Equal, or fecond, but to his in fame.
I, in return, your darling theme will choofe,
And Daphnis' praifes fhall infpire my mufe ;
He, in my fong, fhall high as heav'n afcend,
High as the heav'ns ; for Daphnis was my friend.

MOPSUS.

His virtues, fure, our nobleft numbers claim ;
Nought can delight me more than fuch a theme ;

Which

Which in your fong new dignity obtains;
Oft Stimichon has prais'd the lofty ſtrains.

MENALCAS.

Now Daphnis ſhines, among the gods a god,
Struck with the ſplendors of his new abode :
Beneath his footſtool far remote appear
The clouds ſlow ſailing, and the ſtarry ſphere.
Hence, ev'ry field exalts its chearful voice,
Full of glad melody the groves rejoice ;
Pan, with the Dryads and the Shepherds, ſings,
And ev'ry hill and ev'ry valley rings.
The wolves no more to murder are inclin'd,
No guileful nets enſnare the wand'ring hind ;
Deceit, and violence, and rapine ceaſe,
For Daphnis loves the gentle arts of peace.
From ſavage mountains founds ecſtatic riſe,
And ſhouts of joy exulting to the ſkies :
The rocks, the ſhrubs, emit harmonious ſounds ;
Thro' Nature's wide extent *the god, the god* rebounds.

Be gracious ſtill, ſtill preſent to our pray'r;
Four altars, lo ! we build with pious care ;
Two for the god of ſacred verſe ordain'd,
And two for thee, O Daphnis, we intend.
Two bowls white-foaming with their milky ſtore,
And two with gen'rous olive brimming o'er,
Each year we ſhall preſent before thy ſhrine,
And chear the feaſt with lib'ral draughts of wine ;

Before

Before the fire, when winter's cold invades,
In summer's heat, beneath th' embow'ring shades,
With Chian wine, the facred goblets crown'd,
Shall pour the sparkling nectar to the ground.
Damoetas shall with Lyctian Ægon play,
And celebrate with songs the festive day:
Alphesibæus' steps and wild grimace
Shall imitate the dancing satyr-race.
These rites shall still be paid, so justly due,
When we the survey of our lands renew,
And when the nymphs receive our annual vow. }
While fishes love the streams and briny deep,
And savage boars the mountain's rocky steep;
While grasshoppers their dewy food delights,
While balmy thyme the busy bee invites;
Thy godlike name, thy honours and thy praise
Shall be resounded in unceasing lays.
Such rites to thee the shepherds shall ordain,
As Ceres and the God of Wine obtain.
To hear our pray'rs thou never wilt refuse,
So gratitude shall bind us to our vows.

M o p s u s.

What thanks, what boon can such a song requite!
Can ought in nature yield so sweet delight!
Not the soft sighing of the southern gale,
That faintly whispers o'er the flow'ry vale;
Nor, when light breezes curl the liquid plain,
To tread the margin of the murm'ring main;

Nor

Nor prattling brooks, that plaintive glide along
The rocky dale, delight me as your fong.

MENALCAS.

No mean reward, my friend, your verfes claim:
Take then this pipe that fung the fruitlefs flame
Of Corydon; when proud Damætas try'd
To match my fkill, it dafh'd his hafty pride.

MOPSUS.

And let this fheepcrook by my friend be worn,
Which brazen ftuds in beamy rows adorn;
This fair Antigenes oft begg'd to gain,
But all his beauty, all his pray'rs were vain.

✝✝✝✝✝✝✝✝✝✝✝✝✝✝✝✝✝✝✝✝✝✝✝✝✝✝✝✝✝✝

The Tenth Paftoral of VIRGIL,

Attempted in ENGLISH VERSE.

By the fame.

GALLUS.

TO my laft labour lend thy facred aid,
O Arethufa! that the cruel maid

With

With deep remorfe may read the mournful fong;
For mournful lays to Gallus' love belong.
(What mufe in fympathy will not beftow
Some foothing ftrains in pity to his wo?)
So may thy ftreams unmix'd, and pure of ftain,
Traverfe the waves of the Sicilian main!
Sing, mournful mufe, of Gallus' lucklefs love,
While the goats browze along the clifts above.
Nor filent is the wafte; while we complain,
The woods return the long refounding ftrain.

What grove, ye nymphs, was your conceal'd abode?
What lonely lawn, or folitary wood?
When Gallus' bofom languifh'd with the fire
Of hopelefs love, and unallay'd defire!
For not Parnaffus' heights your aid reftrain'd,
Nor Pindus, nor th' Aonian fpring detain'd.
The pines of Mænalus were heard to mourn,
And plaintive founds along the groves were born;
Kind fympathizing tears the laurel fhed,
And humbler fhrubs declin'd their drooping head;
All wept his wo; when, to defpair refign'd,
Beneath a defert clift he lay reclin'd;
Lycæus' rocks were hung with many a tear;
And round the fwain his weeping flocks appear.
Nor fcorn, celeftial bard, a fhepherd's name;
Renown'd Adonis by the lonely ftream
Tended his flocks.—— As thus he lay along,
The fwains and aukward neat-herds round him throng.

W e z

Wet from the winter maſt Menalcas came;
All aſk the cruel objeɕt of his flame.
The god of verſe vouchſaf'd to join the reſt,
And thus : What phrenzy fires thy tortur'd breaſt,
While ſhe, thy darling, thy Lycoris, ſcorns
Thy proffer'd love, and for another burns!
With him o'er frozen waſtes ſhe wanders far,
Midſt camps, and claſhing arms, and boiſt'rons war.
Sylvanus came, with rural garlands crown'd,
And wav'd the lilies long, and flow'ry fennel round.
Next we beheld the gay Arcadian god;
His ſmiling cheeks with bright vermilion glow'd.
For ever wilt thou heave the burſting ſigh!
Is love regardful of the weeping eye!
Love is not cloy'd with tears; alas! no more
Than bees luxurious with the balmy flow'r;
Than goats with foliage, than the graſſy plain
With ſilver rills, and ſoft refreſhing rain.
Pan ſpoke. And thus the youth with grief oppreſt:
Arcadians, hear, Oh! hear my laſt requeſt:
Oh! you, to whom the ſweeteſt lays belong,
Oh! let my ſorrows on your hills be ſung.
If your ſoft flutes ſhall celebrate my woes,
How will my bones in ſweeteſt peace repoſe!
Ah! had I been with you a country-ſwain,
To dreſs my vine, to tend my bleating train;
Had Phillis, or ſome other rural fair,
Or black Amyntas been my darling care;
(Beauteous tho' black; what lovelier flow'r is ſeen,
Than the dark violet on the painted green!) ;

Theſe

Thefe in the bow'r had yielded all their charms,
And funk with mutual raptures in my arms.
Phillis had crown'd my head with garlands gay,
Amyntas fung the pleafing hours away.
Here, O Lycoris, purls the limpid fpring,
The meadows bloffom, and the woodlands fing;
Here let me prefs thee to my panting breaft,
Till youth, and joy, and life itfelf be paft!
Banifh'd by love, o'er hoftile lands I ftray,
And mingle in the battle's grim array;
Whilft thou, relentlefs to my conftant flame,
(Ah! could I difbelieve the voice of fame!),
Far from thy home, unaided and forlorn,
Far from thy love, thy faithful love, art born,
On the bleak Alps midft chilling blafts to pine,
Or wander waftes along the frozen Rhine.——
Ye icy paths, Oh fpare her tender form!
Oh fpare thofe heav'nly charms, thou wint'ry ftorm!
Hence I will haften to fome defert grove,
And footh with fongs my long unanfwer'd love.
I go —— in fome lone wildernefs to fuit
Euboean lays to my Sicilian flute.
Better with beafts of prey to make abode
In the deep cavern, or the gloomy wood;
On trees to carve the ftory of my wo,
Which with the growing bark fhall ever grow!
Meanwhile with woodland nymphs, a beauteous throng!
The winding groves of Mænalus along
I roam at large; or chafe the foaming boar,
Or with fagacious hounds the wilds explore;

Carelefs

Carelefs of cold.—— And now, methinks I bound
O'er rocks and cliffs, and hear the woods refound;
And now with beating heart I feem to wing
The Cretan arrow from the Parthian ftring:
As if I thus my phrenzy could forego,
As if Love's god could melt at human wo.
Alas! nor nymphs, nor heavenly fongs delight——
Farewell, ye groves! ye groves no more invite!
No pains, no miferies of man can move
The unrelenting deity of love.
To quench your thirft in Hebrus' frozen flood,
To make the Thracian fnows your dear abode,
Or feed your flock on Ethiopia's plains,
When Sirius' fultry conftellation reigns,
(When deep-imbrown'd the languid herbage lies,
And in the elm the vivid verdure dies),
Were all in vain: Love's univerfal fway
Extends to all, and we muft Love obey.

'Tis done—— ye nine, here ends your poet's ftrain,
In pity fung to footh his Gallus' pain;
While, leaning on a flow'ry bank, I twine
The pliant ofiers, and the bafket join.
Celeftial nine! your facred influence bring,
And footh my Gallus' forrow while I fing;
Gallus, my much belov'd! for whom I feel
The flame of pureft friendfhip rifing ftill.
So by a brook the verdant alders rife,
When foft'ring zephyrs fan the vernal fkies.

Let

Let us be gone: at eve, the fhade annoys
With noxious damps, and hurts the finger's voice;
The juniper breathes bitter vapours ronnd,
That kill the fpringing corn, and blaft the ground.
Homeward, my fated goats, now let us hie;
Go home, my goats, the gloomy night is nigh.

✠ ✠✠✠✠✠ ✠✠✠✠✠✠✠✠✠✠✠✠✠✠✠✠✠✠✠✠✠✠✠ ✠✠ ✠✠✠✠✠✠

A VERSIFICATION of the Fifth Fragment of ANCIENT POETRY.

From the Galic or Erfe language.

A piece in the tafte of the celebrated Mr GRAY.

By a Gentleman of Scotland

Dark Autumn now affumes its fading reign,
    The blue-gray mift creeps flowly o'er the hill;
Dark rolls the river thro' the narrow plain,
    And from the uplands burfts the new fwoll'n rill.

On yonder heath there ftands a lonely tree,
    And there, O Connal! thy fad grave is found;
And ftill its falling leaves it ftrews on thee,
    Still by the whirlwind born in eddies round.

Here

Here oft at twilight gray, or purple dawn,
  As o'er the heath the mufing hunter hies,
The sheeted ghoft ftalks o'er the dewy lawn,
  Or haunts the dreary grave where Connal lies.

Thy race, O Connal! who fhall ftrive to trace ?
  Or who thro' ages paft thy fires can tell?
As the tall oak torn from its native place,
  They grew, they flourifh'd, and in thee they fell.

Mournful thy wars, O Fingal! 'Midft the flain,
  Where groan'd the dying, welt'ring in their gore,
There Connal fell! the terror of the plain !
  There fell the mighty to arife no more!

Thy arm a tempeft from the bellowing main,
  Thy fword a meteor in the ev'ning-fky;
Thy height a rock, that overlook'd the plain;
  A glowing furnace was thy wrathful eye.

Loud as a ftorm, thy voice confounding all;
  Dire was thy fword, and eager to deftroy;
Beneath thine arm the mighty warriors fall,
  As falls the thiftle by the playful boy.

As lowring thunder o'er the mid-day fkies,
  Dargo the bold, Dargo the mighty, came;
Dark was his brow, two hollow caves his eyes,
  Bright rofe their clafhing fwords with fparkling flame.

P   Crimora

Crimora——Rinval's beauteous daughter, near
   Her much lov'd Connal.——Could fhe ftay behind!
A bow her fhoulder grac'd, her hand a fpear,
   And loofe her waving locks flow'd in the wind.

At Dargo's breaft the fatal fhaft fhe drew,
   Swift from her arm the mortal weapon flies;
Alas! the erring dart her Connal flew,
   Alas, he bleeds! alas, her Connal dies!

So falls a rock, torn from the fhaggy hill,
   So falls an oak, the glory of the plain.
What fhall fhe do? what griefs her bofom fill!
   " By me is Connal, haplefs Connal, flain!"

All day fhe wanders by fome namelefs ftream;
   Connal my love! Connal my friend! fhe cries;
At night the pathlefs vale by Cynthia's beam;
   For grief, the lovely mufing mourner dies.

The lovelieft pair cold earth doth here inclofe
   That ever flept within her clay-cold womb;
Alone they reft in undifturb'd repofe,
   The green grafs rankling o'er their narrow tomb.

I, mufing in the melancholy fhade,
   The rank weed ruftling to the whiftling wind;
Still mourn th' ill-fated youth and haplefs maid,
   And ftill their mem'ry rufhes on my mind.

A Poetical TRANSLATION of the
Twelfth Fragment of ANCIENT
POETRY.

From the Galic or Erfe language.

R Y N O,   A L P I N.

R Y N O.

HUſh'd are the winds, and paſt the driving ſhow'r,
And calm and ſilent is the noontide-hour ;
The loofe light clouds are parted in the ſkies,
O'er the green hills th' inconſtant ſunſhine flies ;
Red through the ſtony vale with rapid tide,
The ſtream defcends, by mountain-ſprings fupply'd !
How ſweet, O ſtream ! thy murmurs to my ear !
Yet ſweeter far the tuneful voice I hear :
'Tis Alpin's voice, the maſter of the fong ;
He mourns the dead, to him the dead belong ;
Some heart-felt ſorrow bends his hoary head,
And fills his ſwimming eyes ſuffus'd with red.
Why try'd, O maſter of the fong, thy ſkill,
Alone fequeſter'd on the ſilent hill ?

Why

Why like the blaſt that makes the woods complain,
Or wave that beats the lonely ſhore, thy ſtrain?

A L P I N.

The tears, O Ryno! which alone I ſhed,
The ſtrains I ſing are ſacred to the dead.
Tall is thy ſtature on the mountain bare,
On the green plain beneath thy form is fair;
Yet ſoon, like Morar, ſhalt thou meet thy doom,
And the dumb mourner ſit beſide thy tomb;
The hills no more ſhall hear thy jocund cry,
And in thy hall thy bow unſtrung ſhall lie.

Swift wert thou, Morar, as the bounding roe,
As fiery meteors dreadful to the foe.
Like winter's rage was thine, in ſtorms reveal'd;
Thy ſword in fight like lightning in the field;
Thy voice like torrents ſwell'd with haſty rains,
Or thunder rolling o'er the diſtant plains:
Unnumber'd heroes has thy arm o'erturn'd;
In ſmoke they vaniſh'd when thy anger burn'd.

Thy brow how peaceful when the war was o'er!
Like the firſt ſunſhine when it rains no more;
Calm as the moon amidſt the ſilent ſky,
Calm as the lake when huſh'd the tempeſts lie.

How narrow now thy dark abode is found!
Now with three ſteps thy grave I compaſs round;

Great

Great as thou wert, four ftones with mofs o'ergrown,
Thy fole memorial leave thee half unknown;
The lonely tree, where fcarce a leaf we find,
The long rank grafs that whiftles in the wind,
Thefe, and thefe only guide the hunter's eye
To find where Morar's mould'ring reliques lie.
How low is Morar fall'n! alas! how low!
No tears maternal o'er his afhes flow;
No tender maid to whom his heart he gave,
Sheds love's foft forrows o'er his humble grave;
Cold are the knees his infant weight that bore,
And Morglan's lovely daughter is no more.

But who low-bending o'er his ftaff appears,
Opprefs'd at once with forrow and with years?
A few white hairs are o'er his temples fpread,
His fteps are feeble, and his eyes are red.
Thy fire, O Morar, is the fage I fee,
Thy fire,—— alas! the fire of none but thee.
He heard thy martial fame, fupreme in fight,
Of daring foes he heard difpers'd in flight:
Of Morar's fame he heard, why heard he not
The wound, the hero's death was Morar's lot?
O! fire of Morar, ftill thy fon deplore
Weep on for ever, but he hears no more;
Deep are the flumbers of the filent dead,
And low their pillow in the duft is fpread.
No more thy voice he hears with filial joy,
Thy call no more his flumbers can deftroy.

When,

When, in the grave, ah! when fhall morning break,,
The chearful morn that bid's the flumb'rer wake!

Farewell, O! firft of men, untaught to yield,,
Unrivall'd victor in the hoftile field.
The hoftile field thy voice no more alarms,
Nor the dark foreft lightens with thy arms;
To no fond fon defcends thy treafur'd fame,.
Yet fhall the fong preferve thy living name;
The fhining record ev'ry age fhall fee,
And TIME's laft falt'ring accents tell of thee..

✤✤✤✤✤✤✤✤✤✤✤✤✤✤✤✤✤✤✤✤✤✤✤✤✤✤✤✤✤✤✤✤✤✤✤✤✤✤

To MIDNIGHT. An Ode..

By Mr A. E——..

I.

HAil, mufing Midnight, let me rove,
Unnotic'd in thy awful gloom;
While Darknefs wav'ring o'er the grove,.
Involves the day-light's radiant bloom,
I'll dauntlefs ftray, devoid of fear,
Let but the ftars of night appear,

Let

Let but a pale and tranfient gleam
Of moonlight tremble on the ftream :
Then pour, ye tender thoughts, into my mind,
While fwells the long long voice of flowly-rufhing wind;.

II.

And yet why truft the filent hours,.
　　Or give to wo the time of reft,
　　While weaknefs ev'ry fenfe o'erpow'rs,
　　And foft'ning fadnefs heaves the breaft?
Why feek the folitary fcenes
Of melancholy-haunted plains,
Where fancy peoples ev'ry fhade
With ghofts of long-lamented dead,
Whilft no fond friend's grief-foothing voice is near,.
To check the rifing figh, or ftop the ftreaming tear ?

III.

Ev'n now, upon the bed of care,
　　With dread appall'd, the murd'rer lies ;;
Pale Fear erects his rifing hair,
　　The wretch's foul within him dies ;.
As glide the fpectres thro' the gloom,
His eager ftarting fhakes the room ;
Ah ! fhield him Heav'n, the forms advance,.
They fweep along with fudden glance ;
And while the gale blows paft with louder tone,
He views the gufhing wound, and hears the dying groan..

IV.

IV.

Ev'n now intent on Shakefpear's page,
    The youth whom fervid genius warms,
Glows as he reads with godlike rage,
    And feeds on Fancy's fairy charms:
He views the foul of curs'd Macbeath,
And winds along the haunted heath;
Or hears the ghoft of Hamlet tell
In burning words the pains of hell;
Or perch'd with Ariel on the bloffom'd bough,
Beholds the fetting fun thro' crimfon clouds fail flow.

V.

Sleep folds the eyes of keen Difeafe,
    The forrowing voice of Pain is dumb,
The mortal feels unwonted cafe,
    The long-expected flumbers come.
His active pow'rs the god renews,
He fucks at vernal morn the dews,
He marks, as gradual breaks the day,
Health with an eye of pureft ray.
Give all her floating vefture to the breeze,
Mount the light airy cloud, and hover o'er the trees.

VI.

And now perhaps in fleep reclin'd,
    Forgot the cruelty of day,
I rufh upon Dione's mind,
    Her favage fternnefs caft away;

She

She thinks fhe fees around me move,
The gentleft form of genial love;
She blufhing clafps the eager boy,
And checks not his unruly joy:
Hafte, let me realize th' illufive blifs,
O'erpower'd and melting down in each foul-raptur'd kifs.

‡‡‡‡‡‡‡‡‡‡‡‡‡‡‡‡‡‡‡‡‡‡‡‡‡‡‡‡‡‡‡‡‡

A PASTORAL BALLAD.

By the fame.

I.

HOW vain are the efforts of art?
  How vain are the fmooth ftudy'd lays?
Ev'ry language but that of the heart,
  Muft fail in my Phyllida's praife.
How modeft, yet free, is her air?
  Her words with what foftnefs they flow?
She has fill'd ev'ry heart with defpair;
  She has made ev'ry fhepherd my foe.

N

II.

For since she appear'd on our plains,
　　On me she has lavish'd her smiles;
I'm the envy of all the young swains,
　　To supplant me they're fruitful in wiles.
But let me their passions despise,
　　Their proceedings I never will mind,
If my Phyllis approve with her eyes,
　　If my Phillis continue but kind.

III.

I watch ev'ry glance of her eyes,
　　Ev'ry blush that but dawns on her cheeks;
How I tremble if ever she sighs!
　　How I'm raptur'd if ever she speaks!
If she talks, it is heav'n to hear;
　　If she smiles, it is heav'n to see;
How soft, how engaging, how dear,
　　How all over heaven to me!

IV.

My fields, and my orchards are small,
　　Yet planted, and cultur'd with care;
My groves they are lofty and tall,
　　And a sweetness is found in the air.
She admires the increase of my fields,
　　She admires the still gloom of the woods,
The sweetness the healthful air yields,
　　And she likes the wild fall of the floods.

V.

V.

We have wander'd along the green hills,
  Thro' the plains ever vernal with flow'rs,
Thro' the lawns ever gleaming with rills,
  By the banks ever shady with bow'rs;
There my charmer still rais'd such wild strains,
  As wantonly melt in the throat,
Refounding thro' woods, and thro' plains,
  Sweet echoes prolong'd each breath'd note.

VI.

We stray at the dew of the dawn,
  Thro' fields where the west wind has flown,
Collecting the flow'rs on the lawn,
  By the warmth of the gale newly blown.
What beauty is found in their dyes,
  While attended by health thus we rove,
And I see in my Phyllida's eyes,
  Content, soft associate of Love?

VII.

Already our flocks jointly feed,
  They never are separate seen,
Together they sport on the mead,
  And crop the soft herbs of the green:
And hence all the shepherds forefee,
  That Phyllis will quickly be mine;
Oh! thought full of transport to me,
  For the day how I eagerly pine.

The

The CHAIRMEN: A Town-Eclogue.

By the fame.

IN Lothian's fertile fields, whofe ev'ry plain
Luxuriant fmiles o'erfpread with golden grain,
Built by the ancient Picts, Edina ftands;
Rear'd high in air above the level lands,
It emulates the rocks that round it rife,
And feems like them to mingle with the fkies.
Nay, at a diftance, it requires much fkill
To know the city from the tow'ring hill.
But you'll be weary of defcription grown,
Come on then, reader, we'll walk in to town*
Fierce fummer-funs had now dry'd up each ftreet,
And for a wonder all the town fmelt fweet;
The late o'erflowings of the peaceful night
Were robb'd of fmell by the great fource of light;
The fouthern gale impregnated with life,
Pours the full ftink upon the coaft of Fife;
And country-ladies, as they fnuff the wind,
Sigh for the joys that they have left behind :
Now founding bells had, with repeated ftroke,
Proclaim'd aloud that it was twelve o' clock,

When

When two young chairmen, famous for their vigour,
This one *Macewen* call'd, and that *Macgregor*,
Began, oh sad and rueful was their tone !
Their mournful griefs alternately to moan.
First then Macewen spoke; his face all pale,
His mouth all clammy for the want of ale.

M A C E W E N.

The gods, my friend, reject our humble pray'rs,
And laugh at chairmen, and their empty chairs :
Last night my knees, I'm sure, were bent an hour,
The deities befeeching for a show'r.
'Tis, let me fee, a fortnight fince it rain'd,
And all my pockets are of halfpence drain'd;
The cellars where I cramm'd till like to burst,
Are shut against me, and refuse to trust;
Nay, what's most cruel, even mutton-pye,
Delicious dish ! hard fate ! denies supply.

M A C G R E G O R.

Your case is surely bad; but yet I think,
That want of meat is light to want of drink :
Oh say, what direful pangs the man affail,
Who for a fortnight has not tasted ale !
Full fourteen days, the mighty gods can tell,
My drink has been the water from the well.
How often have I curs'd the cloudless sky !
How long shall both the streets and me be dry ?
Behold the bones just starting from my skin,
Alas! the mournful cause is want of gin.

Q   M A C-

M A C E W E N.

Should this fine weather laft, for my own part,
I'll carry chairs no more, but drive a cart;
And ftill to keep my body with my foul,
Inftead of carrying men, I'll carry coal;
I'll change the town for fome fair rural fcene,
Where never chairman or his chair was feen.
Ye footmen, chimney-fweeps of blackeft hue,
Ye dear companions of my youth, adieu !
Farewell, ye blythfome games, I'll grieve your lofs;
Farewell Catch-honours, farewell Pitch and tofs !
Behold yon beau array'd in chearful green,
Lo on his ftockings not a fpeck is feen;
Where now he walks, I've view'd the filth fo thick,
That there almoft his fpindle fhanks would ftick.
Ye chambermaids from higheft windows pour,
Ye gods, o'erwhelm him in a faline fhow'r.
Alas ! I fondly rave, what have I fpoke ?
Thefe things are all referv'd for ten o'clock.

M A C G R E G O R.

Nay, don't defpond, my friend, there's rain in ftore;
Again we'll hear the foaming kennels roar ;
Adown the ftreet they fhall impetuous flow,
Too mighty to be ftepp'd by belle or beau :
For trav'lers fay, and trav'lers feldom lie,
That, fearch the globe all o'er, this town's leaft dry.

MAC-

M A C E W E N.

Your kind reproaches, pray, Macgregor, fpare ;
Like a Macewen I'll my forrows bear ;
With you, my friend, I'll hope for better days,
For great affemblies, crouded routs, and plays :
What tranfport when the great folks trip down ftairs,
And fcreaming beaux, like eunuchs, fqueak for chairs !
" Come, Lady Betty's chair ! Mifs Sufan's here !
" Where are the fellows? fure they'll ftay a year."
When once they've handed in the little fouls,
Away we run, regardlefs of our poles ;
Of the fatigue we furely can't complain,
When the white fixpence well repays our pain.

M A C G R E G O R.

When Digges did Mr Hamlet in the play,
Drefs'd like a provoft on a king's birthday,
That very night five fixpences I got,
Which mended well my breeches and my coat.

M A C E W E N.

The thoughts of thofe dear times my heart revive,
The cart was never made that I will drive.

So ends their fpeech ; when, lo, a fudden blaft
Of wind and rain the beauteous fkies o'ercaft :
A chair is call'd ; in hafte away they trudge,
And bend and fweat beneath a heavy judge.

E C-

ECLOGUE I.

By the Rev. Mr C ———.

Nunc fcio quid fit amor. ——— VIRG.

BY flow'ry banks of Tweed, whofe waters glide
Thro' famous valleys, crown'd with rural pride,
Young Colin led his flock, as fummer gay,
And healthful as the bounteous gift of May.
Yet mourn'd the fwain ; for, pierc'd by fad defpair,
The flave of Love, and its confuming care,
Along the willow-fringed banks he ftray'd,
While fighs the anguifh of his heart betray'd.
Hung o'er the flood a fhady poplar grew,
This, as he lean'd, the falling tears bedew ;
On this he gaz'd, and while his forrows flow'd,
Warm kiffes on the letter'd rind beftow'd.

Ye Albion dames ! to whofe love-darting eyes
The vanquifh'd world refigns bright Beauty's prize,
By love infpir'd, I fing his tender ftrains,
My tale of love the cruel fair difdains ;
Tho' the cold maid my numbers fail'd to move,
In vain I fing not, while your fmiles approve ;

Accept

Accept my verfe: the fav'rite page fhall fhine,
And facred myrtle round my temples twine.

Ye woodland fcenes! where vainly I retire,
Defence from Phœbus', not from Cupid's fire;
Ye fhady beeches! liften to my ftrain,
Infpir'd by Delia, and her proud difdain:
Sad Colin, doom'd her cruel fcorn to prove,
To you, ye rocks! declares his hopclefs love.
Cold-hearted maid! for thee, in early bloom
I wafte neglected, and in tears confume.
In peace retir'd, my happier days were fpent,
In harmlefs pleafure, and in calm content;
On balmy wings each fmiling fummer came,
And found me carelefs by the cooling ftream;
When gloomy Winter vex'd the troubl'd air,
Safe from his ftorms, I watch'd my fleecy care;
At village-feafts, amid the rural throng
I rul'd the dance, and rais'd the fimple fong:
Happy, from forrow and ambition free,
And much too happy, but, O Love! for thee.

All-conqu'ring Love! I feel thy tyrant reign;
Infpir'd by thee, I burn and wafte in vain;
Ye gods! what magic can our hearts fecure,
What art can fhield us from the mighty pow'r!
The feirceft fouls his matchlefs force can move,
And gods themfelves have felt all-conqu'ring Love.
Too well thy nature and thy pow'r I know,
Now haplefs left to unremitting wo:

No

No more from Harmony I hope for eafe ;
Nor flow'ry lawns nor funny field; can pleafe :
All Nature's beauty yields no joy to me ;
For Nature faddens fince de pis'd by thee.

The breath of mildew kills the vernal bloom;
With dire difeafe the harmlefs flocks confume ;
Chill Winter blafts the glory of the year ;
Thy fcorn, O Delia! is the plague I fear.
Sweet are foft flumbers on the verdant plain ;
Sweet cooling fountains to the thirfty fwain;
Sweet gentle funfhine or defcending fhow'rs,
To fervent bees, or to the drooping flow'rs :
Thou, Delia, all my hope, and without thee,.
What's joy, or fun, or life itfelf to me !

Come, lovely nymph ! thy cruel fcorn refign ;
Come, lovely nymph ! and feed thy flocks with mine.
Happy with thee thro' flow'ry fields I'll ftray,
Or wafte, in pleafing toils, the fummer-day ;
Your fnowy flock to frefheft pafture lead,
Or by the breezy fhore, or verdant mead
Irriguous, where the purple vi'lets glow,
The ftrawberries ripen, and the rofes flow ;
There foft reclin'd, and banifh'd ev'ry care,
I'll fing, or wreath with flow'rs thy beauteous hair.

Now all around me breathes the blufhing year,
Prideful the trees their flourifh'd branches rear ;

From fragrant blooms the grateful odours rife,
And rip'ning harveft glads the fhepherd's eyes:
All Nature fmiles, the hill, the flow'ry plain;
Love, only Love, no kind return can gain.

  Come, charming maid! for thee my bow'r is crown'd
With rofes, balmy woodbine breathes around;
O'er the green turf my fpotlefs wool is caft,
And choiceft fruits afford a rich repaft:
Befides, while rival nymphs my favour woo
With gifts, their gifts are all referv'd for you:
Even blooming maids have fu'd my love to gain,'
And am'rous nymphs prefer their gifts in vain;
With me their charms no kind acceptance boaft,
In thine alone all other charms are loft.

  I burn, I burn, as woodland fhades confume,
Conceive deftruftion, and affift their doom:
O when wilt thou thy killing fcorn forego!
When wilt thy breaft an equal paffion know!
Storms ceafe to blufter, and the feas to roar,
Even raging tempefts give their fury o'er;
Would heav'n you too were mutable as thefe,
And could be foften'd like relenting feas!
But, deaf as rocks beat by the founding main,
You frown unmov'd, regardlefs of my pain.

  Ye confcious echoes! vocal through the dale,
To Delia loud proclaim my mournful tale;

On

On all your wings, ye fanning Zephyrs, bear,
And breathe my forrows round the cruel fair;
Her virgin pride my tender verfe fhall move,
And foft compaffion touch her foul with love.
Ah haplefs fwain! thy Delia is not kind,
But ftern and ruthlefs as the winter-wind;
She Colin and his proffer'd love difdains,
And Colin vainly to the rocks complains.
No figh, no tear her killing fcorn difarms;
She claims thy life, the victim of her charms.

I go, I go! compell'd by proud difdain,
Kind death is near to rid me of my pain:
Where o'er the flood projects the rocky fteep,
And hoarfe below is roll'd the grumbling deeep;
From its proud height my wretched weight I'll throw,
And reft in death from Love's tormenting wo.
Adieu, my flocks; adieu, ye groves and plains;
Now ceafe, ye woods, no more refound my ftrains.

E C.

E C L O G U E II.

By the same.

Hic gelidi fontes, hic mollia prata Lycori :
Hic nemus, hic ipso tecum confumerer ævo.— VIRG.

NOW Sol the skies with purple light array'd,
The glories of his weftern throne difplay'd ;
Where the clear ftream, with verdant alder crown'd,
Flows gently murm'ring o'er the channel'd ground,
While all is flufh'd by the departing ray,
Demas and Hylon fram'd the rural lay :
Young Demas o'er the perjur'd Chloris mourn'd,
And Hylon for his abfent Delia burn'd.

Soft as they fung, the fighing groves complain,
The forrowing flocks attentive heard the ftrain ;
With pity mov'd, the filver fwans deplore,
And taught the theme to all the lift'ning fhore;
The lift'ning fhore to ev'ry verfe reply'd,
And zephyrs o'er the bending ofiers figh'd.

O

O thou whom Phœbus and the Nine infpire
With powerful art to ftrike the founding lyre,
To roufe the Britifh youth in war's alarms,
To fire each patriot breaft with Glory's charms,
To call forth virtue by the magic found,
From crouds attentive, and confenting round ;
Accept, O HUME ! and let this myrtle twine
Around thy garland, woven by the Nine :
This humble fhrub would fome protection claim
Among thy laurels rifing unto Fame.
Ye fylvan pow'rs! ye Genii of the grove !
Ye Echoes, vocal with my tale of love !
Ye meads, adorn'd with flow'rs of golden hue,
That fill their cups with tears of ev'ning-dew !
Ye mourning woods, ye weeping fountains, join
Sighs with my fighs, and fhed your tears with mine!
Of Chloris perjur'd loudly I complain,
Hear, and affift this laft, my dying ftrain.
No more the days on golden wings fhall rife,
While bounteous Nature paints the vernal fkies ;
For me no joys fhall purple Autumn bring,
Nor Winter conqueft at the village ring ;
The verdant mountain and the flow'ry field,
The fhepherd's charge no more delight fhall yield ;
With Chloris Nature did her charms difplay,
With her they flourifh'd, and with her decay.
For her, well pleas'd I join'd the rural throng,
The fhepherd's fortune, and the fhepherd's fong;
By her forfaken, thefe delight no more,   •
Nor plains, nor mountains, nor the breezy fhore.

While

While well-known scenes and conscious groves I view,
My passion rages, and my griefs renew.
Say, hapless youths, who Love's disaster prove,
How great the anguish sprung from slighted love!
Chloris! I waste beneath thy proud disdain;
Resound, ye woods, resound my dying strain.

Here, where the green walks lead to op'ning glades,
Cool'd by soft fountains, and embow'ring shades,
Here, hand in hand, with Chloris have I stray'd,
Chloris then faithful to the vows she made.
Here, on the sunny bank, where fairest grows
The silver crocus, and the blushing rose,
I gather'd ev'ry flow'r that seem'd most fair,
And deck'd the garland for her beauteous hair;
Each morn her favour with fresh gifts I sought,
And downy chesnuts from my hamlet brought.
Ah! now these careless joyful days are gone,
Chloris is fled, and I am left alone.
Chloris the shepherd and his gifts disdains,
Resound, ye woods! resound my dying strains.

Where the tall myrtle spreads its branching shade,
On the fair rind I carv'd the vows she made;
Ev'n then I clasp'd her in my circling arms,
And glow'd enamour'd with deceitful charms.
Her faith she pledg'd, invok'd the gods above,
And call'd on all the mighty powers of Love,
She swore, and said, When Chloris perjur'd proves,
Vultures shall fly before the fearless doves;

O'er

O'er the midland fhall boiling ocean roar,
And waving harvefts turn to fandy fhore;
On barren oaks fhall golden apples grow,
And rivers backward to their fountains flow.
Flow back, ye ftreams! and feek your fprings again;
Arife, ye floods! and overwhelm the plain:
Chloris is falfe! no more the dove fhall fear,
Nor barren oaks their fruitlefs branches rear.

Ye pow'rs that over Love myfterious reign!
To you I come, nor let me plead in vain;
For you at midnight fhall my incenfe rife,
With all the pomp of magic facrifice;
Cyprefs fhall wave your flaming altars round,
With lonely weed each image fhall be crown'd;
By moonlight I will cut th' unripen'd ear,
And mournful yew and deadly nightfhade bear;
Libations dire your lift'ning pow'r fhall move,
I'll drink the potion, and forget to love;
While, witnefs to your rites, the filver moon
Eclipfing oft, fhall look with pity down.

I rave! I rave! what charms fuccefsful prove,
Againft the fhafts of all-fubduing love!
Chloris ftill in my inmoft bofom reigns,
Fills ev'ry thought, and burns thro' all my veins;
With flow-diffolving anguifh I confume,
And life is only but a joylefs gloom;
Soon will its care and adverfe frown be o'er,
Demas at reft, and Chloris lov'd no more:

Demas

Demas to filent dreary fhades fhall go,
Where lucklefs lovers reft from human wo:
Farewell, ye flocks! adieu, ye groves and plains!
Now ceafe, ye woods! no more refound my ftrains.

Next Hylon fung, while, from a myrtle fpray,
The nightingale purfu'd her am'rous lay.

Begin, my mufe! the foft Sicilian ftrain,
Sicilian mufes haunt the flow'ry plain.
Now the cool ev'ning fheds its purple ray,
And dewy night fucceeds the fcorching day;
From new-fhorn meads the dufty fwains retreat,
The weary reaper feeks his humble feat;
Beneath the fhade the jovial lab'rers reft,
And ev'ry fwain is with his Sylvia bleft:
Where now, oh! where can charming Delia ftray,
While Love's foft fires upon her Hylon prey?

Begin, my mufe! the foft Sicilian ftrain;
Such am'rous lays a mighty charm contain:
While Orpheus fung, he footh'd the fhades below,
And Hell confenting, mourn'd the poet's wo;
Th'ambitious youth Timotheus could infpire
With love at once, and check the rifing fire;
With fong the Syrens rul'd the lawlfs main,
And mighty warriors bound in magic chain.
By fong, I'll try my Delia's heart to move,
And numbers fhall recall my abfent love:

R   Hark!

Hark! from the spreading oak's aerial boughs,
His ling'ring mate the am'rous ring-dove woos;
From yonder beech th' impatient turtle sighs,
And, see, her lover at the signal flies:
Forlorn, unpity'd, and unheard I mourn;
'Tis night, yet Delia deigns not to return.

Begin, my muse! the soft Sicilian strain;
Come, Delia, come! and bless thy faithful swain.
As Phœbus sunk, the yellow sun-flower mourns,
Shuts up its leaves, and droops till he returns:
As, without genial heat, the tender vines
Decay, and ev'ry with'ring flow'ret pines;
So, far from Delia, love's dissolving flame,
And fruitless sighs destroy my sinking frame:
Absent from thee, what object can delight!
The flocks displease, and sunshine turns to night;
The woodbine-shade its balmy sweets denies,
The drooping lily hangs its head, and dies;
Th' industrious bees neglect their flow'ry toil:
Come, Delia, come! and all around will smile.

Begin, my muse, the soft Sicilian lay;
My song, ye floods, to Delia's ear convey.
Perhaps ev'n now amid your cryftal waves
Her snowy sides the naked wanton laves;
Breathe soft, ye zephyrs, round the gentle fair!
Ye river-nymphs, employ your friendly care!
May no rough touch her tender limbs moleft,
Nor rougher wave insult her snowy breaft.

But,

But, Delia, hafte, thy fimple veftures feize,
Nor give thy beauties to the ruder breeze.
Come, Delia, come ! and let my longing arms
Infold thee, glowing with diforder'd charms.

But whence the fields this fudden verdure wear,
And o'er the plain refounding fhouts I hear !
Soft am'rous whifpers die along the fhore,
And ere he fets, gay Phœbus finiles once more :
'Tis Delia ! Delia, ye immortal pow'rs !
Delia confents to blefs the filent hours :
Ceafe, then, ye gentle mufes ! to complain,
No more refound the foft Sicilian ftrain.

Thus fung the fhepherds at the clofe of day,
The fky ftill blufhing with the ev'ning-ray ;
Safe in the fold they lodge their fleecy care,
And, warn'd by Hefp'rus, to their home repair.

To

-Mrs K----cH of G-----TON.

By the fame.

Quis defiderio fit pudor aut modus
Tam cari capitis? præcipe lugubres
Cantus, Melpomene.   Hor. lib. 1. Carmin.

W Eary'd with Grief's fad office, pleafing pain,
    To join with forrow the confenting voice,
The gen'rous figh, and fympathetic tear,
Forth from the lonely manfions of the dead,
With wand'ring fteps I turn'd, and left the fane,
Where pious grief had led me to difcharge
My mournful tribute, at BELINDA's grave;
To fhed in fadnefs the foft falling tear,   ·
To ftrow the green turf with fweet-fmelling flow'rs,
And fing foft reft to the departed fhade.

    Difconfolate, along the frefh-fhow'r'd bank,
I flowly took my folitary way.
The cryftal brook, which fed the bord'ring flow'rs,
With plaintive murmurs fought the diftant vale;
The curfew, folemn knell of day, prepar'd
The world for reft; the chearful fun had funk ·
His golden orb, and Philomel alone,

                                 Sole

Sole fitting in the neighb'ring grove, purfu'd,
With many a warbled maze, her trilling ftrain.
Down on the dark green grafs I fat reclin'd;
And while ftill Night, in ebon mantle clad,
With filent fteps led forth her folemn train,
Thus fadly to the lift'ning vale I mourn'd.

O fatal day! thou bitter fource of wo!
Which left us poor, bereft of what we priz'd!
O cruel Death! which robb'd the world of joy;
And for BELINDA, comelinefs itfelf,
Soft feeling pity, virtue mildly great,
Wit, elegance, and open-hearted truth,
Left us the cold pale corfe; the dull remains
Of worth returning to her native fkies.

O mournful change! How has Death's killing blaft
Transform'd the rofes of that damafk cheek
To deadly hue! Thofe eyes with wifdom bright,
Which, like two friendly ftars, their bleffings fhed,
Benevolence and peace, to human kind,
How has dark night extinguifh'd all their fire!
That tongue, which with the voice of mufic fpoke,
While more enamour'd ftill, PALEMON hung
In pleafing admiration, as when men
High-favour'd hear defcending angels talk,
How has dumb filence with ftrong magic bound
The pow'r harmonious, never to awake!
That look divine, pervading to the foul;
That elegance of form, refiftlefs, fhap'd

R 3   By

By Beauty's fineſt hand; how has the bane
Of chilling Death each wondrous charm deſtroy'd!
And all ye nobler graces of the mind!
Whom Fancy fails to paint, and mortal tongue
But ill explains by words; how are ye fled
From human ſight! Thou heavenly piety,
Conjugal love ſincere, parental care,
Domeſtic goodneſs, friendſhip, ſocial joy,
Endearing life; kind ſympathy, which falls
The gen'rous tear, and haſtens to relieve;
Good-nature, ſmiling like the golden morn;
Clear ſenſe, and virtue fearful to offend;
Each precious gift which bounteous Heaven beſtows,
To 'thine admir'd, and bleſs the world with good.

O ruthleſs Death! thy cruel hand hath pluck'd
This beauteous flow'r, and rifled all its ſweets!
Relentleſs Death! what ravage haſt thou made
Of boaſted worth, which all the world admir'd!
BELINDA, in the beauty of her youth,
Show'd like the poplar, glory of the grove,
Which lifts the verdant top, and ſpreads its boughs,
Diſpenſing fragrance, till ſome ſtormy night
Shiver its ſtrength, and tearing from its ſeat,
Spread forth the beauteous ruin on the plain.

O early loſt! in the full noon of life,
When ev'ry grace ſhone in its ſummer bloom;
Untimely loſt! while the rich gift of Heaven
Shone bright to all, and with its value won.

The

The fad remembrance only now remains,
Which fondly whifp'ring what BELINDA was,
Recounts to thee, PALEMON ! all her worth,
Renews thy lofs, and on thy fancy preys.
Enamour'd o'er this precious gem you hung,
And drunk in pleafure from its beamy rays :
But in ill-fated hour, rapacious Death,
Like the night-felon, ftole with filent fteps,
And quench'd thy diamond's blaze, and left thee dark,
Forlorn, of all thy wealthy treafure fpoil'd.

No more the fmiling hours on golden wings
Shall pafs rejoicing, nor behold thee gaze
On Beauty's face, enamour'd of her charms;
No more at evening-walks fhall hear the voice
Of conjugal efteem, of piercing fenfe,
Of friendfhip, honefty, and glad content,
In bufy converfe join'd.   Thy pleafing race,
The fruit of faithful love, no more fhall meet
The mother's fondnefs, haft'ning to explain
Th' imploring look; nor friend nor kindred feel
The virtuous tranfport, that endearing blifs,
Which crown'd the focial hour, when gentle peace,
When rofy mirth, and honefty of heart,
When wit refin'd, and gen'rous freedom met.

For now this friendly ftar, which lately fhone
So lovely bright, is fhorn of all its beams :
The beauteous blaze is fet, and chearlefs night
Darkling fucceeds.   Yet know, BELINDA dies'

Only

Only to view; for, like the weftern fun,
She fet to rife with frefh refplendent beams,
In brighter fkies, and fhine with nobler fires;
While Nature's Lord, who wak'd th'immortal flame,
Has rais'd the fplendor, never more to fet.
PALEMON, dry thy tears, and with the eye
Of holy faith look up : this facred truth
Speaks wondrous joy to thy deploring mind ;
Though for a fpace the ftroke of death fhall part
Whom ev'ry wifh and holy tie had bound;
Yet fhall they meet, the long-loft friends fhall meet,
The tender hufband and the loving wife,
And meet, rejoicing they fhall part no more.

Such was my theme, while folemn Night began
Her peaceful reign ; fair Hefperus was fet
In the clear weft, while, with unclouded ray,
Night's emprefs rofe, bright Cynthia, to her throne;
Glad of her filver beams, in hafte I rofe,
And homeward faft explor'd my weary way.

Edinburgh, Sept. 6. 1757.

SONNET

SONNET I.

By the same.

WHen pleafing cares difturb the youthful breaft,
  When ardent fighs fpeak forth the heart's defire,
When hopes and fears confume the hours of reft,
  Then Venus fets the lover's foul on fire.

Then would I fcorn the wealth which many choofe,
  And look on gay plum'd honour with difdain;
Th' infpired mind a nobler aim purfues,
  And Venus' flave fubmits to Venus' chain.

Should fame, or pow'r, or wifdom, plead, to move
  A lover's mind, with all their fpecious fhow,
While Venus fooths me with the fmiles of love,
  Like Paris, ever at her fhrine I bow.

While CELIA here rolls her love-darting eyes,
  Here let me kneel, no other boon I claim;
Beneath the fun the Phœnix burns and dies,
  Beneath her charms I burn with grateful flame.

But fpare, O CELIA ! fpare my tender heart;
  Love, too much love, is all thy fuppliant's crime;
Wound not my breaft with fuch a cruel fmart,
  Nor blaft with killing fcorn my youthful prime.

Sweet

Sweet are thy smiles, O fair-one! and bestow
　New life, beneath the sunshine of thine eyes;
Deadly the shaft of scorn from Cupid's bow,
　And when it strikes the hapless lover dies.

The merchant dreads the rage of winter-seas,
　And fearful cares surround the tyrant's crown;
The mother hears of war with trembling knees;
　I know no danger but in CELIA's frown.

A lover prays, O CELIA! lend thine ear,
　Be kind as beautiful; then shall I joy
A sweeter music than proud arts to hear,
　And for the fairest form my verse employ.

✤✤✤✤✤✤✤ ✤✤✤✤✤✤✤✤✤✤✤✤✤✤✤✤✤✤✤✤✤✤✤✤✤

SONNET II.

By the same.

A Wake, my lyre! thy sadly pleasing strain
　　Shall sooth my anguish, while thy numbers flow;
Awake, my lyre! it fits thee to complain,
　In sounds according with thy master's wo.

Like

Like CELIA's, fweet thy voice, my tuneful lyre,
    And youths and maids attend thine am'rous lay ;
Like CELIA, ftill you feed her lover's fire,
    But yield no hope his torment to allay.

In vain great Hermes deftin'd thee to charm,
    In vain the mufes taught their bard to fing ;
The pow'rs of love the pow'rs of art difarm,
    And all thy magic can no comfort bring.

Phœbus in vain would wake thy joyful found,
    To calm the tumults of a lover's breaft ;
The god of love each captive fenfe hath bound
    In cruel chains, nor gives his victim reft.

Yet fhall thy fad and folemn mufic fay
    How much I fuffer, and how much I love ;
Perhaps fair CELIA may thy fong repay
    With pity, where her charms deftructive prove.

A CONVERSATION with CUPID.

——————————— ὃ βρίφες μὲν
Εσορῶ, φίρον ὃ τόξον,
Πτέρυγάς τε ὃ φαρίτρην.   ANACREON.

ONE day, where winding Liddo ſtream'd,
   As I a-fiſhing ſtood,
I ſpy'd a boy who buſy ſeem'd
   In cutting of my wood.

In haſte away my rod I threw,
   The childiſh thief to ſeize ;
You little raſcal, how dare you
   Deſtroy my growing trees ?

The waggiſh puppy nothing ſpake,
   But ſmil'd, and ſhook a bow ;
Then I diſcover'd my miſtake ;
   O Cupid ! is this you ?

The ſame.   My arrows all are ſpent,
   I have not one to ſhoot ;
And, by your leave, good Sir, I meant
   My quiver to recruit.

I did not know you when I us'd
  Th' uncivil words I fpoke ;
Nor afh, my boy, nor beech, nor oak,
  To you fhall be refus'd.

But will you, Cupid, drop the art
  Which does the world fuch hurt ?
To pierce poor fellows through the heart,
  How cruel is the fport !

See how in Liddo's limpid ftream
  The fportive fifhes leap ;
I'd have you try the wat'ry game,
  And lure them from the deep.

A fifhing-rod I'll make your bow,
  The ftring will be a line ;
For hooks, if arrows points won't do,
  I'll give you fome of mine.

I'd but a bungling angler be ;
  No more on't, if you pleafe ;
Blind as I am, yet can I fee
  You grudge me a few trees.

Take back then what I've got, he faid ;
  Then let an arrow fly :
Deep was the cruel wound it made,
  And deeply did I figh.

S   Keen

Keen as the firft, another ftrikes;
In grief and pain I fled :
Fool that I was, to give him fticks,
Wherewith to break my head !

＊

✤✤✤✦✤✤✦✤✤✦✤✤✤✦✤✤✤✦✤✤✤✦✤✤✦✤✤✤✦✤✤✦✤✤✦✤✤✤✦✤

C U P I D a P A T I E N T.

Amor eſt medicabilis arte.   OVID.

To Dr Taylor, the celebrated oculiſt.

G Reat Sir, a love-fick fwain applies
   To your unerring art ;
By op'ning a blind ftripling's eyes,
   You'll heal an aking heart.

You have fuch an eftabliſh'd vogue,
   He needs fo much your aid,
'Tis ſtrange his cafe the little rogue
   Has not before you laid.

If

If at your chambers he appears,
    Him by thefe marks you'll know,
Arrows in his left hand he bears,
    And in his right a bow.

Give entrance to the wicked elf,
    Though he pretend he's poor ;
For many a man befides myfelf
    Will club to pay his cure.

But as he is a naughty boy,
    You muft take fpecial care,
Ere you your inftruments employ,
    To make him vow and fwear,

By Cytherea's charming face,
    Her chariot and her doves,
Her girdle and her looking-glafs,
    And all the little loves,

That if the bleffings of the fight
    On him your hands beftow,
Soon as he can enjoy the fight,
    He'll archery forego :

Afide his bow and arrows laid,
    His quiver and his darts,
He'll follow fome more lawful trade
    Than that of breaking hearts.

S 2

Affectedly A N A C R E O N says *,
That to be near his lass,
He'd be transform'd into her stays,
Her stockings, shoes, or glass;

Her patch-box, necklace, flow'rs of gum,
Gown, apron, capuchin,
Nay, pearl-powder would become,
To beautify her skin.

* Εγὼ δ' ἐσοπῖρον ἐην,
Οπως ἀἡ βλἰπης με.
Εγὼ χιτὰν γινοίμην,
Οπως ἀἡ φορῆς με.
Ύδωρ θἰλω γινἰσθαι,
Οπως σὶ χρῶτα λὐσω.
Μύρον, γὺναι, γινοίμην,
Οπως ἰγὼ σ' ἀλἡφω.
Καὶ ταινίν δὶ μαςῶν,
Καὶ μάργαρον τραχἡλῳ.
Καὶ σάνδαλον γινοίμην,
Μόνον ποσὶν πατἦν με.

But

But I would undergo a change,
 (Vain, giddy, lovely Sue,
To gain thy favour,) far more ſtrange,
 And far more painful too.

What charms finery has for thee,
 Alas! too well I know,
And therefore wiſh, ſome god would me
 Transfigure to a beau.

Since empty titles to thy pride
 Would no ſmall joy afford;
To be created, I'll abide,
 (So pleaſe the king), a lord.

To more I will ſubmit ere long,
 And, to get an eſtate,
I'll lick gold-duſt with fawning tongue
 At ſome great ſcoundrel's feet.

   *

The RESPECTFUL LOVER.

LET others more forward behave,
  With eafy familiar air,
For my part, I cannot believe
  That brifknefs and brafs win the fair.

Of her I adore, ev'ry glance
  A tender confufion infpires ;
Her charms fo majeftic at once
  Invite, and yet awe my defires.

How often, in vain, the whole day
  My paffion to fpeak have I ftrove,
Then taken fome round-about way
  To tell her how ardent my love ?

How I fondled and flutter'd the rofe
  To-day in her breaft that fhe wore ;
She certainly could not fuppofe
  I ever once thought on the flower.

I threaten'd to pluck off its head,
  Attempted its leaves to deftroy ;
For when a feign'd ftruggle we made,
  Her bofom I touch'd by the by.

Alone

Alone when I gaze on her charms,
　How fain would I ravifh a kifs ?
How fain clafp her fhape to my arms ?
　But I dread fhe would take it amifs.

Tho' modeft perhaps to a fault,
　Tho' bafhful and aukward my air ;
Yet my heart with true paffion is fraught,
　And I will not fubmit to defpair.
＊

✢✢✢✢✢✢✢✢ ✢✢✢✢✢✢✢✢✢✢✢✢✢✢✢✢✢✢✢✢✢✢✢✢

The MATHEMATICIAN

To His Mistress.

WHY heaves my bofom up and down ?
　My pulfe and nerves why ftir fo ?
In *Capricornus* is the fun ;
　But I would lie in *Virgo*.

Ah cruel *Solid,* thou alone
　Art of my woes the root !
Contact with me why do you fhun,
　And play the *Afymptote ?*

No

No more by you will I be teaz'd;
'Tis but a cruel joke,
To keep me always electris'd,
And waiting for the *shock*.

A chart of thee I lately drew;
But, ah! from neck to knee,
Terra incognita was you
In my Gunography.

Ev'n algebraic rules can't shew
A method to reveal
That *unknown quantity*, which you
So anxiously conceal.

It rather would I find, I swear,
Than the north-western road,
The circle or triangle's square,
Or even the longitude.

To trifle in this great affair
Both dangerous and silly is;
For life is short, none of us are
Perpetuum mobiles.

Coquettish therefore cease to be,
Nor catch at all at random;
But give your heart and hand to me,
Q. *E.* *D.*

The

The S I G N S difcontented.

THey queftion Jove, why he had not
In heav'n a ftock of females laid in?
He but one woman there had brought,
Who was (provoking!) ftill a *Maiden.*

Frankly the *Ram* confefs'd that he
Had often caft a *fheep's eye* at her.
Aquarius acknowledg'd fhe
Had often made his teeth to *water.*

The *Bull* would have the god to know,
Either he would no longer ftay there,
Or if he did not get a cow,
In faith he would *Pafiphae* her.

Poor *Virgo* how to pleafe them all
Being really at a lofs to know,
To *th'Archer* faid, I fear I fhall
Have more than *two ftrings to my bow.*

But if to you I fhould prove kind,
The reft would make the fame requeft ;
Shall I be with a *Scorpion* join'd,
Or take a *Cancer* in my breaft ?

Nor

Nor fhould my coynefs you difpleafc;
  This was the purpofe of my birth;
Not only you to tantalize,
  But all the ftargazers on earth.

Not for the fun or moon, but me,
  Aftronomers make fuch a pother;
The truth is, they would rather fee
  My *heav'nly body* than another.

For fuch a peep they fhould not hope,
  But mind their own terreftrial laffes;
My petticoats they'll ne'er fee up,
  With all their telefcopes and glaffes.

LYRO.

An elegy on a BASS VIOL, broke
by a fhort-fighted gentleman, who fat
down upon it.

Vitaque cum gemitu fugit indignata fub umbras.

I Had a bafs —— Ah me ! it is no more ;
Dumb are thofe ftrings fo ready once to roar.
To gloomy hell the heav'n-taught fpirit flies,
And here the head, and there the body lies.
Poor breathlefs thing ! if ever I forget
Thy once lov'd mufic, may I fhare thy fate.
No, gentle bafs, like WILLIAM fhalt thou be,
Of glorious and immortal memory.
Can I forget thy reverend grimace,
Thy folemn form, and philofophic face ?
Can I forget thy foul-inchanting fong,
Sweet, though fonorous, delicate, though ftrong ?

With

With wanton notes your voice ne'er brib'd the ear,
Nor were old Cato's morals more fevere.
Like Cato too you fled from folitude,
And thought fociety your greateft good.
Whene'er you fung, you help'd another's ftrain,
And was to fiddles what he was to men.
Unhappy viol! why before thy time
Did the fates fnatch thee *humming* in thy prime?
To thee untimely death if they decreed,
Why did they fever from thy trunk thy head?
Nor Whig nor Tory was you when alive,
Nor arm'd rebellious in the *forty-five*;
Could not the Sifters other death afford
Than that which honour'd many a rebel Lord!
Tell, O Melpomene! in mournful ftrain,
By what foul means my lucklefs bafs was flain.

A plain, good, fimple, honeft man there was,
Nor friend nor foe to this unhappy bafs;
Blind men, and thofe that have their eyes, between,
Nature had plac'd him in a purblind mean:
Tir'd with the tuneful labours of the day,
As on a chair your bafs repofing lay,
Thy evil genius made this man appear.
The bafs he faw not, though he fpy'd the chair.
Souce down he fits —— when, lo! ftrange founds were
　　heard,
And fad hoarfe groans the purblind mortal fcar'd.
With foul embrace your viol was opprefs'd ——
I can no more —— yourfelf may guefs the reft.

Curs'd

Curs'd be the wretch, from whence foe'er he come ;
Accurs'd his eyes, but more accurs'd his bum.
A fhrew's fharp nails have many a vifage flea'd.
And Englifh boxers vanquifh with their head :
But of all mortals ftigmatiz'd in verfe,
He firft has murder'd with a monftrous ———
With horror I, O bafs ! thy fate muft view ;
Not only death, but ignominy too !
Had fome fair fhe, with bum as white as fnow,
Dealt thy devoted neck the fatal blow,
Pleas'd to the laft you'd dy'd in chearful mood,
" And kifs'd the ——— juft rais'd to fhed thy blood.*"

* Pleas'd to the laft, he crops the flow'ry food,
  And licks the hand juft rais'd to fhed his blood.   Pope.

T   An

An EPISTLE from Phillis to Chloe,

Giving an account of the fmuggling-trade carried on by the Ladies with the Eaft-India company's fhips that came into Leith road in 1758.

A FRAGMENT.

Juft fafely landed from a ftormy fea,
Pleas'd your commands, dear Chloe, I obey;
A various groupe for your amufement draw,
What things I fmuggl'd, and what men I faw.

Firft know, dear girl, though in each Indian fhip
A fkilful merchant may perhaps buy cheap,
To them no women fuch incitement drew,
'Twas not our chief, but fecondary view;
'Twas not the goods, but men we meant to try,
And thither went to barter, not to buy.

Soon as I came aboard, I was addrefs'd,
And to a cabin pull'd with am'rous hafte.

Here

Here china bowls in juſt gradation riſe,
And ſilks and ſtuffs glare on my dazzled eyes.

Struck with the ſight, and with a dram of rack,
I ſoon, too ſoon, fell proſtrate on my back.
What boots it me the conſequence to tell
To you who can imagine it ſo well ?

The road to pleaſure much the maid miſtakes,
Who grants her favours to the city-rakes ;
In the obſcene debilitated race,
A want of vigour vies with want of grace :
Unlike the ſailor from the Indian land,
From ſoft delights for many a month reſtrain'd ;
In mighty ſtreams his long-ſtopp'd love muſt flow,
" It boils, and wheels, and foams, and thunders thro'."*

My ſailor bold, when I was going 'way,
In every pocket ſlips a pound of tea ;
In fineſt muſlins wraps my legs and thighs,
And cups and ſawcers round my middle ties :
This hand receives a charming Indian fan,
That an old palſy'd Lilliputian man,
Who ſeem'd to blame the bargain I had made,
And diſapproving, ſhook his aged head.
        *   *   *   *   *   *   *   *   *   *   *

* See Thomſon's Spring, and there the deſcription of a river
in flood.

                    *
                T 2   ADVICE

Advice to a young POET.

Parce, puer, ftimulis, et fortius utere loris. Ovid.

THE world efteems fuch men as are of ufe,
But fneers at fuch as only can amufe.
Who does not fmile when he beholds advance,
Him who to fiddle teaches, or to dance,
Or ev'n the noble fcience of defence ?
The art of thofe who on the ftage excel,
Is furely next to that of writing well;
Yet their profeffion is the leaft exempt
From th' agonizing ftigma of contempt.

Juft fo (but would 'twere not my lot to fhow it)
Is he receiv'd who's nothing but a poet :
He's much carefs'd, and much admir'd, 'tis true;
But players, fiddlers, fencers, are fo too.

Be then inftructed in this ufeful leffon,
Avoid to be a poet by profeffion.
The ivy which ne'er unfupported fprings,
But round the oak for its protection clings,
Should teach each bard to feek the friendly aid,
Of fome more ferious beneficial trade.

But

But don't imagine I am fo fevere,
As to infift you fhould all verfe forfwear.
If you fplenetic, rainy be the day,
Better in verfe fome foolifh thing effay,
Than lofe your temper and your cafh at play.
But not too often write, nor yet too well,
If in aught elfe you purpofe to excel :
For 'tis a truth, though not unlike a riddle,
That one may play too well upon the fiddle.

Ev'n in the fimpleft and moft ancient days,
Alas! no honour waited on the bays.
Homer, whom all your connoiffeurs admire,
As being of bards the venerable fire,
Was, if the writers of his life fpeak true,
Precifely what an Irifh harper's now *.
For he, ftone-blind, and miferably poor,
With harp on fhoulder went from door to door,
And there whole hours unintermitting play'd
To idle fervants for fome broth and bread ;
Or elfe the naughty children to divert,.
Would in the nurfery employ his art.
But if the mafter of the houfe inclin'd,
With hearing mufic to unbend his mind ;
For his delight he tun'd his choiceft ftrains,
And got perhaps a fhilling for his pains ;
Which he receiv'd with a God blefs you, Sir,
And fo was gone to feek as much elfewhere.

* See Blackwell's life of Homer, and there the defcription of
an *aoides*, or bard.

VERSES

VERSES written in a blank leaf of PRIOR'S POEMS.

MATTHEW PRIOR, to me, 'tis exceſſively plain,
   Deſerves to be reckon'd the Britiſh Fontaine ;.
And Mr Fontaine can never go higher
Than to be admir'd as the French Matthew Prior.

 Thus when Eliſabeth deſir'd,
  That Melvill would acknowledge fairly*,
 Whether herſelf he moſt admir'd,
  Or his own ſov'reign, Lady Mary?

The puzzled knight his anſwer thus expreſs'd :.
In her own country each is handſomeſt.

 * See Sir James Melvill's Memoirs.

 *

I M I-

IMITATION of a FRENCH EPI-GRAM, pasted up in several places at Paris in 1759.

Batteaux plats à vendre,
Soldats à louer,
Ministres à pendre,
Genereaux à rouer.

O France! la sex femelle,
Fit toujours ton destin;
Ton bonheur vient d'une pucelle,
Ton malheur vient d'une catin.

L ET us, since all our expeditions fail,
Our troops to hire, our boats expose to sale;
While those in power a just chastisement feel,
Belleisle the gallows, and Contades the wheel.
In vain, O France, thy legislature strove
From state-affairs the women to remove;
Such the unalterable course of things,
Thy fate must always hang on apron-strings.
Sad the vicissitude we're undergone,
A strumpet loses what a virgin won.

●

VERSES

VERSES to Miss * * * *

Written in a blank leaf of the IRISH POEMS.

WHO can unmov'd of Dargo's daughter read,
Of Connal's love, or Minvane the maid ?
Sweet as the vernal zephyrs was their breath,
Their breasts like snow that floats upon the heath.
Of their bright eyes, tho' keen, yet mild the power,
Like stars, whose lustre vibrates through a shower *.

But where, in times so barbarous and old,
Charms so divine could Highland bards behold ?
Sure the unpolish'd *daughters of the hill*,
Could not their mind with such ideas fill.
No : Highland bards, when they sat down to write,
Summon'd th' assistance of their second sight.
Its magic bade, before their wond'ring eyes,
The loveliest of our modern fair-ones rise ;
From her of beauty they their notions drew,
And so describ'd prophetically — you.

* See the Poems, p. 35. &c.

The

The REFORMED CHURCH.

Nec tamen interea rauc.e, tua cura, palumbes,
Nec gemere aëria ceſſabit turtur ab ulmo.

To the tune of *The birks of Invermay.*

WHile other churches, with ſuccefs
    Inftruct men how to live and die,
The infolence of vice reprefs,
    And guide them to th' realms on high;

Ours fhall improve the common tunes,
    Change all devotion into fhow,
Clothe the precentors with black gowns,
    And make each church a very beau..

What tho' fanatics join to blame
    The guilded defk or painted pew,
And in a holy rage exclaim,
    Sure each man fits in a vain fhew * ?

Nor fear when, from religious fpite,
    They plot the downfall of your dove ;
For beaux and beauties fhall unite,
    To guarantee the bird of love.

But fay, what has he in his mouth ?
    It looks unfeemly at firft view ;
Would he gulp down fome pill uncouth,
    Or does the bird tobacco chew ?

* Sure each man walks in a vain fhew,
    They vex themfelves in vain; —— *Pſa.m.*

Yet

Yet fay, why on the pulpit's top
   Was the dear creature perch'd alone,
There folitary left to mope,
   And his unhappy fate bemoan?

Two clergymen, auftere and grave,
   O'er this collegiate charge are plac'd ;
Then, honour'd Rulers, by your leave,
   We'll have a pigeon for each prieft.

I joy to fee the clerk appear,
   Proud of his fweeping black difguife ;
But why do not the beadles wear
   Ecclefiaftic liveries?

The man who to the playhoufe goes,
   Will fee thofe who the candles fnuff
Have yellow lining to their cloaths,
   Turn'd up too with a yellow cuff.

Since folks of fafhion won't fit nigh
   To their men-fervants or their maids,
Erect a footmens gallery,
   As in the playhoufe, o'er our heads.

Tickets you likewife fhould devife,
   And ftop collections for the poor;
Elfe you can never advertife,
   No money taken at the door.

To

To M O N E Y.

Te ſpeſtem ſuprema mihi cum venerit hora,
Te teneam moriens deficiente manu.—— TIBUL.

O MONEY! MONEY! I too plainly ſee
 That in good earneſt I'm in love with thee ;
When I alone thy beauteous form ſurvey,
Do not my eyes my tender thoughts betray ?
Does not my trembling hand thy perſon ſeize,
And eager graſp thee with an am'rous ſqueeze ?

 No lover can more grievouſly repine
At Chloe's abſence, than I do at thine :
And well I may ; for, when depriv'd of thee,
I can enjoy no other company.

 The lover's ſenſes equal throbbings feel,
Whether he ſees his fair in diſhabille,
Or when full dreſs each heighten'd beauty ſhows,
To rival belles and complimenting beaux ;
Juſt ſo on you my eyes enamour'd ſtare,
In whatſoever figure you appear ;
If, as a guinea, you eclipſe the ſun,
If, as a ſhilling, you eclipſe the moon,
Altho' he be the glorious god of light,
And ſhe the ſilver majeſty of night.

 Nor is m' inconquerable paſſion leſs,
When you in paper whimſically dreſs ;

Tho'

Tho' others at fo thin a garment laugh,
And think your reputation not quite fafe.

Their own opinions lovers often drop,
And thofe their miftreffes embrace adopt;
My Prefbyterian fcruples you remove,
And teach ev'n Popifh fover'eigns to love;
Both *James* and *Charles* have I *chang'd* with pain,
And often wifh'd *th' old Stuarts back again.*

Tho' many lovers hate the blaze of light,
And hold their affignations in the night,
When fleep and filence the creation hufh,
And day extinguifh'd fpares the virgin's blufh;
I won't receive thee darkling to my arms,
But in broad day explore thy Sterling charms;
Left fome vile *whore*, with frontifpiece of *brafs*,
For my true love fhould undetected *pafs*;
And I, as Jacob was of old, be bit,
And not fair Rachel but blear'd Leah get.

Old Cato, fay the writers of his life,
Sent to a childlefs friend his fertile wife;
I'll lend thee too, and fo far imitate
The Roman; but my friend muft not forget,
Mine are the *yellow boys* ye procreate.

But when with me, think not to lead the life
Or of the French, or of the Britifh wife;
Who unprotected roams, to thofe a prey,
By force who ravifh, or by wiles betray:
Much of the Spanifh caution I approve,
And with a padlock will fecure my love.

On the death of Marſhal KEITH.

KEITH then is fall'n! What numbers can there flow,
What ſtrains adequate to ſo great a wo!
Ev'n hoſtile kingdoms in dark pomp appear,
To ſtrew promiſcuous honours o'er his bier.
Hungaria gives the tribute of the eye,
And ruthleſs Ruſſia melts into a ſigh:
They mourn his fate, who felt his ſword before ;
And all the hero in the foe deplore.

What muſt they feel for whom the warrior ſtorm'd,
Whoſe fields he fought, whoſe ev'ry counſel form'd !
Brave Pruſſia's ſons depend the mournful head,
And with their tears bedew the mighty dead :
Sad round the corſe, a ſtately ring they ſtand,
Their arms reflecting terror o'er the land;
With ſilent eyes they run the hero o'er,
And mourn the chief they ſhall obey no more ;
A pearly drop hangs in each warrior's eye,
And through the army runs the gen'ral ſigh *.

* This piece appears to have been wrote before the accounts
that M. Keith's funeral obſequies were ſolemnized by the Au-
ſtrians had reached the author ; a circumſtance which he would
probably have converted to very good purpoſe.

U   Great

Great FRED'RIC comes to join the mighty wo;
Eternal laurels bind his awful brow;
· Majeftic in his arms he ftands, and cries,
Is KEITH no more? and as he fpeaks, he fighs;
In filence falls the fable fhow'r of wo;
He eyes the corfe, and frowns upon the foe:
Then grafping his try'd fword, the chief alarms,
And kindles all his warriors into arms.
Revenge, he cries, revenge the blood of KEITH;
Let Auftria pay a forfeit for his death.
They join, and move in fhining columns on;
Germania trembles to Vienna's throne.

But CALEDONIA o'er the reft appears,
And claims pre-eminence to mother-tears:
In deeper gloom her tow'ring rocks arife,
And from her valleys iffue doleful fighs.
Sadly fhe fits, and mourns her glory gone;
He's fall'n, her braveft, and her greateft fon!
While at her fide her children all deplore
The godlike hero they exil'd before.

Sad from his native home the chief withdrew;
But kindled SCOTIA's glory as he flew;
On far Iberia built his country's fame,
And diftant Ruffia heard the SCOTTISH name.
Turks ftood aghaft, as, o'er the fields of war,
He rul'd the ftorm, and urg'd the martial car.
They afk'd their chiefs, what ftate the hero rais'd;
And ALBION on the Hellefpont was prais'd.

But

But chief, as reliques of a dying race,
The KEITHS, command, in wo, the foremoſt place;
A name for ages thro' the world rever'd,
By SCOTIA lov'd, by all her en'mies fear'd;
Now falling, dying, loſt to all but fame,
And only living in the hero's name.

See ! the proud halls they once poſſeſs'd, decay'd,
The ſpiral tow'rs depend the lofty head ;
Wild ivy creeps along the mould'ring walls,
And with each guſt of wind a fragment falls ;
While birds obſcene at noon of night deplore,
Where mighty heroes kept the watch before.

On Mem'ry's tablet mankind ſoon decay,
On Time's ſwift ſtream their glory ſlides away ;
But, preſent in the voice of deathleſs Fame,
KEITH lives, eternal, in his glorious name ;
While ages far remote his actions ſhow ;
And mark with them the way their chiefs ſhould go ;
While ſires unto their wond'ring offspring tell,
KEITH liv'd in glory, and in glory fell.

The End of the FIRST VOLUME.